MW00833850

BITTER ASHES-BOOK THREE

ROCK, PAPER, SHIVERS

SARA C ROETHLE

Copyright © 2016 by Sara C Roethle

All rights reserved.

No part of this book may be reproduced in any form or by any electronic or mechanical means, including information storage and retrieval systems, without written permission from the author, except for the use of brief quotations in a book review.

❀ Created with Vellum

1

The cold wind stung what was visible of my face, and my hands and feet were numb despite the thick gloves and heavy duty winter boots. As far as the eye could see in any direction was crisp, pure white, almost blinding as the sun made its slow descent toward the horizon. I stood alone, musing over everything that had gotten me to this point, camping out in a frozen wasteland, contemplating summoning gods.

It had taken us weeks to get to our location. Weeks of hiding from our enemies while we traveled through the larger cities. Weeks of plotting our next step. Weeks of waiting for the key to rear its ugly head in an attempt to possess me again. We'd made it all this way without conflict. I shouldn't have been surprised since we'd taken so many precautions, but still, by this point, I expected things to go wrong at every turn. More surprising than our success so far, was that the key had remained dormant within me.

Mikael appeared by my side, staring out at the cold landscape ahead of us as the breeze played with his long, auburn hair. "Are you ready?"

I shook my head. "No."

I rubbed the slight bump of my belly, still not fully believing I was growing a child inside me. My winter clothing was all cinched up around me, so my pregnancy didn't show, but the entire group knew regardless. Sophie had a big mouth.

"Freyja is, among other things, the goddess of child-birth," Mikael reassured, placing a hand on my shoulder. "She will not harm you or your child."

I turned and raised an eyebrow at him, though my eyebrows were mostly covered by the black hood of my jacket. While I wore a top of the line, full-length, micro-down coat, plus many layers underneath to keep me warm, Mikael had only added a heavy, fleece lined, knee length coat to his normal Viking-esque gear. His dusky red hair whipped about freely in the icy air, yet he seemed unfazed. I was freezing even with all the layers. Camping out in the Arctic Circle was no joke.

"She's an ancient goddess," I countered, "one who left our people long before you were even born. You have no idea what she'll do."

Mikael smirked. "No, I don't, but you know I wouldn't tell you that your child will be safe if I didn't think it was true."

"Because of our oath," I agreed.

Mikael rolled his strange, amber eyes. "I wouldn't lie to you about such a thing, even with a blood oath hanging over my head."

I sighed, not because I thought he was misleading me, but because I believed him. The past few weeks had been trying. I'd finally been reported missing back in the States, but luckily still had fake identification from Diana. Many of Mikael's people, living safe within the Salr, had never possessed any real forms of identification, so we'd had to purchase a batch of fake IDs for them. Never mind that Mikael already had *a guy* in place to make the transaction go smoothly, and had around ten different personas in place for himself, all with passports, bank accounts, and backstories. Some even owned property.

We'd done much of our traveling by train, with me gritting my teeth the entire time, waiting for the cops to storm in and take us all away. Mikael had been the one to keep me calm through it all, oddly enough, and I'd really come to depend on him to keep the panic away.

Alaric and Sophie had been there for me too, but they were both a little more blunt, a little less tactful. They said exactly what they thought, which usually wasn't very comforting, though I appreciated it in a whole other way.

I turned to see Alaric waiting in the distance near our camp. He wore a more modern coat like mine, and a stocking cap over his long, black hair. Even from the distance I could tell he was smiling at me, I could *feel* it. Alaric might not be the best with comforting words, but he offered me partnership. We could both be worried together about ourselves and our child, and we could both be brave together. At that moment, if I didn't have Alaric's bravery helping me along, I probably would have called off the whole thing. I wasn't fit to summon gods . . . but then again, who was?

Mikael walked by my side as we started back toward the tents. The dense snow beneath our feet crunched, but didn't give way. I'd slipped and fallen on my butt on some of the harder-packed patches more times than I'd like to admit, far less graceful than any of my companions.

As we reached Alaric, Sophie and Aila came into view, both in full winter gear with their hoods pulled up. Aila looked gargantuan, but dangerous with the added layers on her already tall, muscular physique. I just looked like a fat penguin.

The other members of our small group, Faas, Tabitha, and James, waited inside the large tent that was our main base. The snow mobiles we'd used to reach such a remote area were parked around the tent, covered by fitted tarps, but otherwise ready for a fast escape.

We hadn't wanted to risk bringing any more of Mikael's people into our plan, so it was just the eight of us. We needed to be as unfindable as possible.

Many had voted against even bringing James. He was the weakest link without his memories. The arguments had ended though as Mikael pointed out that James was the only one who could create heat from nothing. It was a useful backup skill when camping on the frozen tundra.

I reached Alaric and stepped into the cradle of his arms, feeling some of the tension leak out of my body at his nearness. If Freyja didn't work out, we'd be using Alaric and Sophie to summon Bastet. I really hoped Freyja worked. I had no desire to meet a cat-headed war goddess.

I looked to Aila, who we'd be using to summon Freyja. All we needed was a bit of her blood. Aila looked nervous, her eyes a little too wide, and I knew it wasn't the prospect of slicing her arm open that had her worried. She'd suffered countless injuries over her long life, but it wasn't every day you met your patron deity.

Faas appeared from within the tent, just as bundled up as me. As executioners, denizens of death, we were much stronger in the magical department, but slightly lacking in the physical. In other words, we were a lot more prone to the elements.

Faas' white hood covered his blond swatch of hair and eyebrows, leaving only his eyes and nose visible. His eyes no longer held intense hatred for me, but they were still wary. His job was to step in and drain my energy if the key took over again, and I didn't blame him for being nervous about it, and I was still just as nervous around him. Even though he was built smaller than any of the other men, and tended to be less aggressive, he'd mastered skills I'd only recently found out I even had, and he knew how to use them to kill, maim, and control. He couldn't heal though. That little quirk was mine alone, but he had a little quirk too. He could drain energy from those who were uninjured. I could only steal from someone who was already near death, or from a weakened human. Faas had been draining my energy for weeks, keeping me weak enough to prohibit the key from using me to murder everyone.

We'd also kept me away from any corpses so I couldn't get a quick boost, just in case, but the key was still a force all on its own. Even without anyone to drain, it could do a great deal of damage before running out of juice, despite Faas draining my energy.

Still, the key hadn't been present in my mind, except for the occasional emotion leaking through. It was deep in hiding, which made me even more nervous than when it was trying to take over. At least when it tried to take over, I knew what it wanted. When I had learned from Mikael how to shield my thoughts and emotions, the key had learned too. It had built a brick wall between us, letting me know that if I wouldn't let it in on my plans, it wouldn't let me in on its plans either. Of course, I had a feeling it could still *hear* everything that was said, so it probably knew what we were planning with Freyja. Either it agreed with the ritual, or it was waiting for the right moment to pop in and cause chaos.

"Is everything prepared?" Mikael asked as Faas went to stand near him.

Faas nodded, though the gesture was almost imperceptible in his thick coat. "We'll begin the ritual as soon as the sun sets."

We all nodded in agreement, because there was nothing else to do. We were about to use my connection to Yggdrasil, the World Tree, to pull one of the old gods through into our world. If we succeeded, we would ask for her aid. It would be her choice whether she helped us, as there was nothing we could really do to compel her.

We were banking on the small chance that Freyja was a magnanimous goddess. My hopes were not high. I couldn't claim to know much about the old gods, but I knew one thing for certain. No one does anything for free.

2

The thick wool blanket between my body and the ice didn't do much in the way of warmth, and sitting so close to Aila only increased my lack of personal comfort. She wasn't a warm and fuzzy person at the best of times, and her nervous energy was making me itch and sweat beneath my coat.

I would have complained, but even with my discomforts, I was in a better position than most everyone else. Aila and I sat in front of a large fire built in a circular pit James had melted in the ice. The fire illuminated the darkness around us, but only so far. Glancing out in any direction, there was only pure blackness dotted by occasional distant stars. Though the moon was full, clouds obscured much of its light.

Aila and I sat on the blanket by ourselves, while everyone else stood on the other side of the fire, watching us like we might sprout second heads any moment.

Worry creased Alaric's brow, while Sophie just looked bored. Since I had discovered long ago that Sophie's bored face was actually her worried face, I gained little confidence from either of them. Heck, even Mikael looked worried. Next to him stood James, who continuously glanced over his shoulder, like we might be attacked at any moment. He was probably right.

Faas moved to crouch beside Aila, while Tabitha stood behind him, holding an ornate chalice, and a wicked looking, curved blade. Tabitha wore a coat similar to her brother's, the white fabric, nearly the same color as her long hair, blending in with the surrounding snow. She handed Faas the blade as he held his hand out for it, then crouched to hold the chalice underneath Aila's bare, outstretched arm.

I inhaled sharply and turned away as Faas sliced into Aila's forearm, then glanced back to watch her vibrant blood flow into the chalice. The liquid looked dark with only the firelight to illuminate it, flowing across her pale skin like ink.

Aila turned to me. "I hope you know what you're doing," she said flatly in her heavily accented, deep voice.

I tried to smile encouragingly, but really I had no idea what I was doing. We were basing our actions on legends Mikael had read about in a really old book. The ritual was based around using one of the leaves from

Yggdrasil, the World Tree. None of us had ever actually performed such a ritual, since Yggdrasil had been destroyed long before any of us had been born, even Mikael. To many, the tree was nothing more than legend.

Even though I was the youngest amongst us, I'd managed to touch Yggdrasil in person, sort of. My spectral form had traveled back in time, leaving my body behind, but I'd still had the power to unintentionally drain energy from the tree. The power enabled me to return to my body, where Alaric and Mikael were, and to take us all back home from Viking times.

It was not a fond memory for me, because in that moment I'd realized I truly was *death*. The key might have influenced my actions, but *I* was the one that had nearly killed the tree without even trying. More frightening still, was that it had felt amazing.

Not only had some of that power remained within me, connecting me to Yggdrasil forever, but the key was also originally a part of Yggdrasil. The key's existence within me strengthened that connection, or so we'd hypothesized. The tree's untimely death, centuries after the time I'd seen it, created the Norns as they are now, in individual forms, but it also created residual chaotic energies of destruction. In other words, the key. It was as much a part of Yggdrasil as the fates.

Faas took my hands, drawing me out of my thoughts. He guided them toward the fire, close enough to burn. I winced, but held my hands steady above the flames as he pulled away.

Tabitha stood with the chalice full of blood clenched firmly in her gloved hand. She circled behind us, then crouched at my side opposite Aila. I closed my eyes, wanting nothing more than to retract my sore hands. The blood Tabitha poured over them actually came as a relief. It dripped from my skin, sizzling in the fire as it hit, but I barely heard it.

With the touch of blood and fire, my body came alive. Not only did my human senses seem more keen, I was hit with a sudden symphony of emotion. I could sense Alaric's anxiety and Mikael's apprehension. James' fear and frustration. I didn't have time to ponder my new clarity as Tabitha began to chant in Old Norsk over my bloody hands.

As her words dipped up and down in the cadence of an ancient chant, my entire body began to tingle with energy, enough to make me dizzy and a little sick. The key reacted, like I'd been terrified it would. I wasn't sure if it was to Tabitha's words or the blood. Maybe both. I'd never reacted to just blood before. Usually I needed the corpse that went with it.

My hands began to throb like they were filled with too much blood, and I realized that I'd leaned forward enough to completely encase them in the flames, yet they didn't burn. Tabitha continued to chant, while everyone else watched on silently.

Something was thrumming in my chest, but it wasn't my heart. I could feel energy building toward . . . something. I started to panic, worried the key was about to take over like it had done when it first retreated into my body. The energy reached its apex, throwing my head back as it surged upward.

There were a few silent moments where everything seemed still, and I couldn't hear over the ringing in my ears. Once I was able to breathe, I brought my head forward to see the veins in my arms lit up like molten fire. The air around my face shimmered with gold. At first I couldn't tell why, then my eyes focused on the night sky around me. The branches of a great tree formed in the air above me, shining like the sun. *Yggdrasil.*

I could no longer sense nor see anyone around me, just the tree. I wanted to reach out and touch the shining branches, but felt frozen in place, a prisoner to the power that had taken me over. As I continued to stare up at the branches, a bright bolt of light, like a giant shooting star, touched down on one tiny twig at the top of the spectral tree. As soon as it hit, I could sense an immense presence, the likes of which I had never felt.

It shot downward, traveling through the branches of the tree toward my face. I screamed as it came barreling toward me, but at the last minute, it veered down a lower branch and sped toward Aila. It hit her like a Semi truck, throwing her from the blanket to land on the hard ice with a thud.

The moment the energy hit her, the entire tree winked out of existence, and my hands, still in the fire, began to burn.

I screamed and withdrew my hands as everything came back into focus.

Alaric appeared at my side. "How do you feel?" he asked frantically. "Did it work?"

I turned wide eyes to him, holding my burned hands away from my body. I shook my head, not because I thought the ritual didn't work, but because I had no idea what the hell had just happened.

I looked over my shoulder to Aila, who was being helped to her feet by Mikael. She seemed stunned, but unharmed.

I gazed into Alaric's eyes. "Did you see that?" I asked, half-hoping it had all been a figment of my imagination.

"The tree?" he questioned. At my nod, he replied, "Honey, that tree is going to be emblazoned in my memory until the day I die."

I turned my gaze as Faas came to crouch on my other side, while Alaric wrapped his arms comfortingly around me.

"Aila?" I questioned. She'd seemed fine, but now she was mumbling something to Mikael behind us.

"She's fine," Faas replied, as he looked me up and down, likely probing with his magical senses to see if my energy was still the same after the strange occurrence. "You seem unchanged as well," he added finally.

"But whatever that was that came through the tree hit Aila," I argued. "I thought it was coming straight for me, but it veered from its course and hit her."

Faas raised his pale eyebrows. "Something came through the tree?"

I nodded, and turned to Alaric for verification. He *had* to have seen it.

Alaric frowned. "I saw only the tree, then Aila was suddenly knocked aside. Still, if whatever you saw intentionally went for Aila, perhaps Freyja attempted to join us after all."

We all moved to look back at Aila, who still stood in the darkness with Mikael. They had been joined by Tabitha.

Faas stood and approached them. "She doesn't seem any different," he commented as he glanced over Aila once again.

"It felt like whatever hit me bounced off," Aila replied, her deep voice seeming loud in the quiet night.

"Then we have failed," Faas replied somberly, his shoulders slouching in defeat.

I squeezed my eyes shut as a moment of panic hit me, then was gone. We would simply have to try again. The key's presence would *not* remain within me forever. I was still *me*.

Mikael left Aila to approach me. At 6' 5", he was one of the few people around that could make me feel small. Well, him and Aila.

"How do you feel?" he asked, concern clear in his voice. "Did the key react, or was that all *you*?"

I shook my head. "I don't know. It felt like it might have, but it was washed away as the tree formed. I think it was Yggdrasil's remaining energy within me that created the golden tree, and maybe the key too."

"The key was originally part of Yggdrasil," Mikael replied. "You might not be far off in your assumptions, but that doesn't explain why the ritual didn't work in the end."

"But why would the key even allow me to use it like that?" I asked, finally getting to my feet with Alaric's help. "You would think it would want no part in summoning one of the old gods, since they are the only ones powerful enough to separate it from me. *That* wasn't me controlling the key. That was me being taken over by something else. I was just along for the ride."

"Perhaps the key wants to be separated," he mused with a small smile. "It *did* seem to have more power as a separate entity. As things are, it will likely die with you."

I frowned. I'd considered that little metaphysical aspect more than I'd like to admit. The Norn had told me I could end the key by ending my life, and my child's. It was almost selfish to stay alive. Then again, I'd still be leaving everyone in the middle of a war. Estus would likely kill my companions once the key's threat was eliminated, and he would continue being a tyrant over his portion of the Vaettir.

Still, we were the ones who'd forced both Estus' and Aislin's hands. We'd taken the potential for bloodshed up a notch, throwing the two clans more fiercely into a competition they had begun on their own. I wondered how they would react to finding out the key was no longer a physical object. Would they go back into their hidey-holes, content that at least their enemies wouldn't possess such raw power, or would they still try to use me somehow? Perhaps they'd just band together to completely eliminate the threat I might pose.

I shook my head as Alaric gave me a tight squeeze. We'd sure muddled things up since our original plan. We'd gone from wanting to just give the key to Aislin, to starting wars and summoning old gods.

"You seem tired," Alaric commented.

I nodded. I *was* tired, physically, mentally, and emotionally. Having Faas constantly draining a small measure of my energy took its toll. With the added inconveniences of the cold, and the botched ritual, I was ready to sleep for a week.

"We'll try again tomorrow," Mikael assured, startling me because I'd been so deep in thought, I'd forgotten he was still beside us.

Sophie and James waited in the shadows on the other side of the fire. Observing the whole situation silently.

"Let's go to bed," I mumbled.

Alaric nodded, moving just one arm around my waist so we could walk side by side away from the others. I couldn't wait to climb into my insulated sleeping bag, shielded from the cold air by our ridiculously expensive winter tent. My hands ached enough that I was afraid to look at them, and I probably still had remnants of Aila's blood on me. I was too tired to attempt washing it off with icy water, and I had no doubt the contact would increase the pain.

We climbed into the tent, and Alaric zipped it up behind us. The space inside was small, leaving just enough room for our double sleeping bag. I sat on my butt while Alaric helped me out of my coat and boots, avoiding my hands.

"Do you want to bandage them?" he asked, finally taking them tentatively in his grasp. "The burns don't look bad, but it might ease the pain."

I shook my head, barely able to keep my back erect. "Sleep now please."

With a small smile, Alaric helped me into our cushy cocoon, then climbed in beside me.

He rested on his back so I could spoon against him with my head on his shoulder. I buried my face against his neck, trying not to think about the key's presence, threatening to ruin the intimate moment.

"Maddy?" Alaric questioned softly.

"Yes?" I asked with my lips against his warm neck, breathing in the familiar scent of his skin and hair.

He was silent for a moment, then sighed, "Nothing. Rest well."

Normally I would have pushed the matter, but I was too bone tired to try. Instead I shut my eyes and let my mind spiral off into oblivion, because it was a heck of a lot more comforting than reality.

❄

I AWOKE to the sound of the tent unzipping, but felt disoriented. With a start, I realized it was still dark, Alaric was still beside me, and someone else was unzipping our tent.

Without thinking, I reached for the large, sheathed knife I kept near my pillow, just in case, as Alaric finally awakened. We both sat up quickly, ready to face the person now leaning into our open tent.

"What the hell are you doing?" Alaric asked of the dark form.

Tension leaked out of me at his tone. This was obviously someone from our camp. I couldn't see a thing in the darkness, but with Alaric's catlike night vision, he probably saw them clearly.

"*Sophie*," he demanded when there was no reply.

"Sophie?" I questioned, leaning closer to the dark form.

Alaric held me back. "Something's wrong."

As my eyes adjusted, I could see Sophie staring at us, but she wasn't speaking.

She leaned a little closer to peer at me. "That was a very rude summoning, child," she said in a tone of voice I'd never heard coming from Sophie.

"Oh shit," Alaric spat, "Do you think . . . " he trailed off.

My mind caught up to his way of thinking a moment later. "Oh *shit*," I echoed.

Sophie glared at us. "I would discontinue your disrespectful way of speaking immediately, if I were you. Now get out here." She disappeared from the opening.

We scrambled out of our blankets and out into the cold night air, quickly donning our coats and boots as we went. Sophie was obviously not Sophie anymore, something I might have found hard to believe if I hadn't experienced a sort of possession myself previously.

Once we were all out of the tent, we stood in a triangle with Alaric and I both staring at Sophie, and Sophie tapping her foot on the ice impatiently.

"Freyja?" I questioned, my voice tinged with disbelief.

Sophie rolled her eyes. "Freyja no longer answers the calls of her children, girl, and she's not who you need regardless. Most call me the Morrigan, though I go by many other names, and I have come to *your* call."

"What?" I gasped.

No one from the other tents had stirred yet, and I wasn't sure if we should be keeping our voices down for privacy, or if we should be shouting from the rooftops to wake everyone and tell them Sophie had been possessed.

Sophie/the Morrigan seemed confused. "You summoned Yggdrasil itself to light my path, child. Do not tell me you did so by accident."

Alaric was looking at his sister like she was some sort of monster. "This better not be permanent," he interjected.

Sophie glared at him, and it was so much like a

normal Sophie glare it was unnerving. "Your sister will not be harmed," she replied dispassionately. "I would not disrespect Bastet in such a way." She turned back to me. "Now tell me why I'm here."

Her eyes sparkled in the moonlight. I had a feeling she knew a lot more than she was letting on, like she was testing me . . . or toying with me.

My heart thundered in my chest, making it difficult to breathe. I was facing down a goddess, and regardless of her actual intentions, she was obviously not happy. It did not bode well.

"We were trying to summon Freyja," I explained weakly. "We need her help."

Sophie smirked. "You expect the help of the gods, when you have clearly forgotten us?"

I cringed. I'd heard legends of the Morrigan, and I wasn't even sure that she was a *god*, yet here she was.

"We had no other choice," I explained.

Sophie took a step closer to me, really *looking* at me. "There is a secondary energy within you," she observed. "What have you done? I will not have any daughter of mine turning herself into an abomination."

"Daughter?" I questioned, feeling even more confused.

I distantly heard the sound of another tent unzipping. Someone was coming to see what the commotion was.

Sophie smiled. "You truly have strayed far from your roots, my child, and I'm here to bring you back to them."

Her comment didn't quite make sense to me. Here she was acting like she had no idea what was going on, followed by an assumption that she knew quite a bit about me.

The figures of Faas and Tabitha became clear as they approached us, followed by everyone else in our party.

"Wha—" Faas began, then stopped as his eyes darted right to Sophie. "*You're* not Sophie."

Sophie sneered. "How very observant of you." She took in everyone as they came to join us, then shuddered in irritation, reminding me of a bird settling its feathers. "If you all don't mind, I would appreciate a moment alone with my daughter."

Alaric stepped beside me and wrapped an arm around my shoulders, obviously unwilling to leave me alone with the Morrigan. Mikael came into view as he stalked around Sophie, observing her like she was an animal up for auction.

Sophie/the Morrigan frowned and met my eyes. We stared at each other, as she seemed to look into my very soul. I was still stuck on the fact that she'd called me *daughter*.

"Consort with your *man*," she said as a cold smile played across her face. She was ignoring everyone around us, her eyes remaining firmly on me. "I will take a moment to find my bearings in this much changed world."

I nodded a little too quickly. Alaric watched his possessed sister, looking worried as she turned and walked off into the darkness. I didn't blame him, I was worried about Sophie too, despite the Morrigan's reassurances.

"I can't believe it worked," Faas breathed as soon as the Morrigan had taken Sophie's body out of sight.

Mikael seemed pensive, so I turned my full attention to him, with Alaric's arm still wrapped around me.

"What is it?" I asked, wondering if he knew more about the Morrigan than the rest of us.

Mikael frowned. "I'm just not entirely sure why the Morrigan would be the one to answer our call. I wasn't even under the impression that she was a goddess."

The cold was seeping into my bones, and I felt wary being out in the darkness. The Morrigan could have returned to watch us and we might never know. Of course, Alaric would probably smell her if that were the case.

I gnawed on my lip. The Morrigan claimed I was her *daughter*, which as far as the Vaettir were concerned, simply meant descendant, and not even in the most literal sense of the word. There was no actual blood relation, but calling them our ancestors was the simplest way of voicing that information.

"If she's not a goddess," I whispered, "then what is she? How did she travel through Yggdrasil?"

Mikael took all of us into his gaze. "As far as the legends are concerned, the Morrigan is either a witch, some sort of fairy, or both. She was in this world more recently than the old gods, though she disappeared countless centuries ago. Regardless, as far as the stories are concerned, she's not very nice."

"The stories seem accurate," Alaric mumbled.

I sensed fear from Tabitha, surprising me. She was incredibly timid for someone who grew up amongst our people. It was easy to forget that not all Vaettir were as ruthless as the ones I was used to. "What if she's not here to help us? What if she wants the key?" she whispered.

I let out an abrupt laugh, more of an expression of the tension I was feeling than anything else. "Well," I replied, "she'll have to cut me open and sever it from my very being if she wants it for herself."

Tabitha's pale eyes met mine, letting her thoughts show through before she answered, "That's what I'm afraid of."

I caught my breath at the thought as Alaric squeezed me a little tighter. What if she really was there for the key, and I was just a mortal shell getting in her way? How do you stop an ancient witch or goddess from cutting you open?

The only answer I could come up with was, *you don't*.

3

The Morrigan wasn't gone for long, returning within twenty minutes. I could sense the first light of morning not far off, and my bones ached with tiredness, but there was no way I was going back to bed until we figured all of this out. In reality, I probably wasn't going back to bed period, but I'd soothe myself with comforting lies in the meantime.

We all stood waiting by the rebuilt fire as she approached, the firelight illuminating her slender form. Our eyes met. It was just as unnerving seeing someone else looking out at me from Sophie's eyes as it was the first time when she'd practically climbed into our tent.

As she closed the distance between herself and our group, I noticed she walked differently too. Sophie's gait was very direct. Graceful, but aggressive. The Morrigan walked with a slow sway, almost seductively. There was something reptilian about her. The way she moved sent a chill down my spine.

"May we speak in private now?" she asked, her tone making it clear she hadn't appreciated being kept waiting.

"I go where Madeline goes," Alaric answered for me.

The Morrigan/Sophie arched a dark brow at me, her pale face seeming to glow in the firelight. "You let a man speak for you?"

I grabbed Alaric's hand and gave it a squeeze. "Only when I agree with what he says."

The Morrigan sighed. "*You* brought me to this place, not anyone else here," she snapped. "You summoned me with fire, and a sacrifice of blood, and now you cannot be troubled to allow me a private audience?"

I let out a shaky breath. She had a point. I really didn't want to be alone with her, but I wanted her out of Sophie's body sooner rather than later. If Sophie had to deal with being possessed, I could deal with a few minutes alone with the scary witch goddess.

"Fine," I replied before I could think better of it.

Alaric's hand convulsed around mine at my answer. He glanced over at me. "Are you sure?"

I met his eyes and nodded. "If Bastet requested a private audience with you, would you tell her no?"

Alaric was clearly unhappy, but he let go of my hand and nodded for me to go, earning himself a big bag of bonus points.

The Morrigan/Sophie nodded, then turned and

walked back in the direction she had come, expecting me to follow. Everyone else looked as worried as I felt. Their emotions crept over me, making me even more anxious to walk out into our dark, snowy surroundings. I crossed my fingers that at the very least, I wouldn't slip on the ice and embarrass myself in front of my alleged ancestor.

Pushing my worries to the back of my mind, I turned from the group and hurried to catch up to the Morrigan's side as she glided across the hard-packed snow. I felt clumsy next to her serpentine grace, but I felt that way around normal Sophie too, so it wasn't much of a change.

Her dark hair flitted about in the breeze as she asked, "Why have you chosen such an inhospitable environment?"

I watched my feet as we continued to walk. Our surroundings were nothing but white, with scraggly vegetation here and there. Everything was snow as far as the eye could see, which wasn't far in the darkness.

"We're hiding," I explained.

"From whom?"

I took a deep breath as I pondered the best way to explain it. "Basically from all of the Vaettir of the largest two clans."

"Why?"

I was getting tired of walking on the cold, hard ground, and I was getting hungry. The small life inside me demanded more nourishment than I would normally need, and I felt enormous guilt any time I denied it. Still, I did my best to remain patient.

"There exists a charm that was part of Yggdrasil," I explained, starting from the beginning. "When the Vaettir destroyed the tree, the Norns were formed. The leftover dark energy formed a tiny key. The ones after us want that key."

The Morrigan/Sophie laughed for some reason I didn't understand, then nodded as she stopped walking and turned to face me. "I remember that day," she explained. "Your brethren took away the gods' mode of transportation between worlds. You'd think they would have been more grateful to those they were modeled after."

I shrugged. "I wasn't there, so I can't really defend why they did it."

She took a step closer to me. "And yet, you have touched the tree. There is a part of it within you, else you would not have been able to summon me here."

I gulped. I glanced over my shoulder for some form of reassurance, but we'd walked far enough that our camp was entirely out of view. I turned back to meet the Morrigan's cold stare.

"I have touched Yggdrasil," I admitted. "One of the Norns pushed me back in time, not physically, but a part of me traveled there."

"There's more," she observed. "Tell me the rest."

I looked down at the ground. "The charm I

mentioned, the dark energy left over when Yggdrasil was destroyed . . . " I trailed off.

The Morrigan gasped, showing the first real surprise I'd seen on her. "It's within you, isn't it? I knew I could feel it. This is wonderful. We can reopen the gates between the worlds!" She grinned. "Balance will be restored at last."

Her sudden shift to excitement left me reeling. I didn't want to reopen the gates to the old gods. Heck, I could barely comprehend that such gates existed. I just wanted to get rid of the key, while living to tell the tale.

Her eyes narrowed. "I see that is not your intent," she accused.

I shrugged. "We were trying to summon Freyja because we thought she might be compassionate to our cause. I don't want this energy inside me any longer. It took me over entirely before, and all it wants is power and destruction."

The Morrigan seemed to withdraw herself from me, deep in thought. I shivered and wrapped my arms around myself for several minutes while she continued to ponder our predicament.

Finally, her eyes lit up as she came to a conclusion. "We will take the energy from within you, and use it to regrow Yggdrasil. You will be free, and we will restore the natural order. You are wrong to think it only wants power and destruction. It wants chaos. The thing you call the charm is the embodiment of wild magics, and the concepts of luck and chance. War and destruction may come naturally to it, but they are not all that it signifies."

My heart skipped a beat. I wanted to press the *you will be free* comment, but I needed to actually understand the rest before making any real decisions.

I opened my mouth to speak, but she was so excited she didn't seem to notice. She clapped her hands together. "First, I must find a suitable host," she mused. "I would not use one of the children of the gods any longer than necessary."

I opened my mouth again to ask a million questions at once, but suddenly Sophie/the Morrigan shut her eyes and went limp. I darted forward to catch her before she hit the snow.

Cradled awkwardly in my arms, she opened her eyes. Her brow wrinkled.

"Sophie?" I questioned.

"Care to explain why you're cradling me like a child?" she asked, uneasy.

"Um," I began, licking my chapped lips. "You were possessed by the Morrigan."

Sophie pulled away from me and stood. She brushed off her already clean clothes like a cat smoothing its fur. "Come again?" she asked incredulously.

"The Morrigan came through the tree and possessed you," I stated, waiting for her reaction.

Her eyes narrowed. "The Morrigan? I always thought she was just a legend, not a goddess."

"We should get to camp," I advised, hoping for

backup when I explained everything that had happened to Sophie.

She startled and looked around us, as if just then realizing we were standing alone on the frozen tundra. With a look of distaste, she nodded her agreement, and began walking in the direction of the camp without me having to tell her which way it was.

By the time we neared the smell of woodsmoke, the first light of morning had descended. I stifled a yawn, longing to go back to sleep, though I now doubted more than ever that it would happen.

Alaric jogged toward us as we came into sight. If I would have jogged on the snow, I would have broken an ankle, but he did so effortlessly, his feet barely making a sound.

"She's Sophie again," I explained as he reached us.

He let out a long sigh of relief, then swept his sister up in a hug. She struggled and fought him off, then huffed and smoothed her hair.

"Why the hell did she choose to possess *me*?" she questioned. "She could have taken Maddy, or Aila, or anyone actually standing near the ritual."

"Well," Alaric began, "she wanted to *talk* to Maddy, so she wasn't really an option."

Sophie glared at me as if it was all somehow my fault. I lifted my hands in defense. "Don't shoot the messengers."

Sophie sighed and turned back to her brother. "I didn't do anything horrible, did I?"

He shook his head. Just the fact that Sophie thought she'd done awful things while she was possessed made my mind jump back to Mikael's assessment of the Morrigan. He was the one who would likely have any more relevant details on her, so he was the one I needed to speak with.

I walked away from Alaric and Sophie, only to have them both jog to catch up as I approached the fire, which had been rebuilt even larger while I was gone, as if to ward away any more spirits. Everyone had remained awake, and now Aila, James, Faas, Tabitha, and Mikael all sat gathered around the fire for warmth. Something was cooking near the edge of the fire in a large pot.

I looked down at Mikael as he leaned forward to stir the lumpy brown stew. Stew for breakfast. *Yummy*.

"I take it Sophie is Sophie again?" Mikael asked.

I nodded. "The Morrigan is gone, but I'm pretty sure she'll be back. I'd like you to tell me all you know about her before she returns."

He grinned, then patted an empty space on the blanket beside him. "Story time it is!"

Relieved Mikael had shifted back to his normal, joking self, I took a seat beside him. Alaric sat on my other side. Sophie walked across the fire to sit near Aila, who had the hood of her coat cinched over her mane of blonde hair, leaving only her eyes and part of her nose visible.

"There are many accounts of the Morrigan, from many different sources," Mikael began. "Some call her a goddess, some a witch, and some label her a member of the *Tuatha De Danann*, the Celtic fairy folk."

He shifted into a more comfortable position as he continued speaking. "The only thing most accounts seem to agree on, is that the Morrigan is vindictive, a woman scorned. Sometimes she is described as a single woman, sometimes as three, sometimes portrayed as the maiden, the mother, and the crone. In many myths, she's a shapeshifter, changing between the three female forms, as well as the form of a crow. The crow form chooses who will die on the battlefield."

"Well she thinks I was made in her image," I interrupted. "So the death thing kind of fits."

Mikael nodded. "As does your ability to heal."

Well *now* he really had my attention. No one had been able to explain how I was an executioner, but also a healer. The two "gifts" seemed counterproductive.

"Go on," I pressed.

"In early myths, before the Morrigan became more of an ominous figure, she was a bringer of both life and death, keeping the balance. She was a protector of the land, and in some tales, was the earth herself. It was only in the later stories that she was portrayed as a bitter old witch."

"I wouldn't let her hear you say that," I cautioned as the gears began to turn in my head.

Perhaps I really was descended from the Morrigan, if the early stories were true. Just as Alaric, descended from a goddess of war, was skilled in combat and tactical thinking, and Mikael, descended from a god of deceit and treachery, was skilled in manipulation, I might have gained my skills from a goddess of life and death.

Tabitha moved to begin filling wooden bowls with stew. The meat inside looked brown, probably beef, making my stomach churn uncomfortably. My pregnancy had given me a taste for red meat, even though years of not eating it made me sick at the thought. Still, I took the offered bowl. If baby wanted beef, baby would get beef.

I felt almost cozy sitting by the fire, enveloped in the scent of woodsmoke, with a bowl of hot stew warming my hands through my gloves. The comforting illusion was shattered as I noticed the blood stain on the blanket beneath me. It was Aila's blood from the ritual. She seemed dejected this morning, and I wondered if it was because her goddess had rejected her call.

A sudden thought dawned on me. "The Morrigan claimed she wanted to regrow Yggdrasil to restore balance to the land."

Everyone suddenly seemed uneasy, and no one would meet my eyes.

"Why isn't anyone looking at me?" I questioned, not getting why such a notion would scare my companions.

Alaric placed a hand on my leg. "Maddy, when a goddess of death says she wants to restore balance to the land, you should be afraid. When she says she wants to regrow a tree that would allow the old gods to come and go as they please, you should be terrified. Think about it. Life as we know it would cease to exist."

My mouth formed an 'oh' of understanding. Suddenly the stew in my hands seemed even less appetizing. While balance sounded like a good thing, the Morrigan's version of balance might not be what one would expect. She might be even worse than Estus and Aislin combined, and I'd brought her here. Any disasters that might occur would be firmly placed on my head. I could only hope it would remain attached to my shoulders long enough to deal with the fallout.

"So what do we do?" I asked of no one in particular.

"She's here now," Mikael answered. "There's no undoing it, so we should try to move forward as planned. We knew our actions would have grand consequences from the start, so we cannot truly complain when those consequences aren't what we expected. She may not be Freyja, but the Morrigan is still a force to be reckoned with. She could make a formidable ally, and we need all the allies we can get."

I nodded. "So we try to bring her around to our way of thinking. She already wants to free me from the key, so we're halfway there."

Alaric gave my leg a squeeze at the new information. I turned to see him smiling. "If we can manage that much," he commented, "we can worry about the rest later. Separating you from the key takes priority."

Aila snorted, drawing everyone's attention to her. She hunkered further down into her coat.

"Is there a problem?" Alaric questioned.

Aila snuggled her arms tightly around herself, but didn't comment, seeming to regret her snort.

"If you have concerns, then voice them," Sophie pressed, compassionately rather than angrily. It wasn't a tone I heard often from Sophie.

Aila frowned. "Thinking of only the next step, and only how things affect Madeline, has not gotten us very far. Instead of fighting, we are hiding in the snow with our tails between our legs."

Mikael laughed, bringing everyone's attention to him. He grinned in Aila's direction. "What Aila is so eloquently trying to say, is that she hasn't gotten to kill enough things. We promised her war after many years of inaction, and she's seen little of it."

I sighed, not agreeing with the sentiment. "I'm going back to bed," I announced as I stood.

"It's morning," Aila argued.

Alaric stood with me. "I'll join you, in *bed*," he purred lasciviously.

Aila grunted in annoyance, but Alaric only smiled down at her. "There *are* a few things more exciting than battle," he teased. "Perhaps you should try them sometime."

Aila began to lunge forward, but Faas put a hand on her arm, holding her back. He was grinning, as was Tabitha. Something told me that teasing Aila was a favored pastime amongst the group of Vikings.

I urged Alaric forward before Aila decided to kill him, but I couldn't help my grin.

It's funny, just when you think the world has stolen away all your smiles, they tend to come back in the direst of times.

4

Over the next few days, we bided our time, waiting for the Morrigan to return in her new host. Then we waited some more. Finally, on the third night, a woman appeared. She had long, fiery red, curly hair, and dark brown eyes. Her skin was pale, a little too pale, and lightly freckled. She was tall and lithe, with narrow hips and little meat to her. She would have been beautiful in a gaunt sort of way if she didn't look so much like a corpse.

Alaric and I were the only ones who hadn't gone to bed when she arrived, and suddenly I was kicking myself for wanting to stay out by our warm fire to look at the stars. On the other hand, since I knew she had no problem with letting herself into our tent while we were sleeping, maybe staying up had been the wise choice.

The red haired woman approached and sat by the fire, settling the loose, black fabric of her clothes around her. Her dress was partially covered by what could only be called a cloak. Her clothes looked vaguely medieval, but were crafted out of modern day fabrics with fine stitching. She waited as I observed her, staring at us with her dark eyes.

"Are you the new Morrigan?" I asked hopefully, because otherwise some crazy woman had found us in the middle of nowhere, and hoped to share our fire.

She nodded as she tucked her legs a little more firmly around her side. "I apologize for leaving you for so long. It took time to find an acceptable host in a stage where its soul had left it, but it still had not begun to rot. I cannot maintain anything with another soul in it for long, unless the vessel has welcomed me as its guest."

I cringed, since she'd basically just said that she'd taken over a dead body, though I supposed it was better than her stealing a live one.

"Aren't you cold?" I asked, not knowing what else to say.

She glanced at the dark snow around her, then shook her head. "This body is dead. It feels very little."

Well that was an uncomfortable thought, though I was a little envious that she didn't have to feel the cold. Alaric remained silent beside me, allowing me to do the talking, though his eyes were cautiously glued to the Morrigan.

The Morrigan began playfully swooping her hand through the fire, back and forth, quick enough to not let her skin burn.

I cleared my throat.

Her eyes met mine. "I forget how impatient children can be," she mused. "If we must speak, tell me more of this war. I haven't tasted war in quite some time."

I took a deep, even breath, picturing the Morrigan as a crow flying over the battlefield.

"There have only been small skirmishes so far," Alaric explained, letting me off the hook. "Madeline was to use the deaths to destroy the key, but complications arose."

I shivered. *Complications* was one way of putting it. A total lack of will power and follow through on my part was another.

The Morrigan's gaze went distant. "It was a sound plan, if only you'd known exactly what you were dealing with."

The way she spoke made it seem like we *still* didn't know what we were dealing with. If that was the case, I'd have to argue, since what we were dealing with was now a part of me.

Her eyes suddenly snapped to mine. "You were chosen for a reason. The fates may be scattered and unorganized, but have no doubt, it was fate that brought you together with such a divine force. This is not entirely a curse, though you may view it as such."

I wrapped my arms tightly around myself. I didn't believe in fate. Too many screwed up things had happened over the course of my life for me to believe they were *meant* to happen. No, I believed in *choice*, even if an alleged deity was arguing otherwise.

"Let's see," she continued, eyes once again going distant. I was beginning to get the impression she wasn't entirely sane. "First, we'll need to choose the location for the final battle," she continued. Her eyes returned to mine. "You will need enough energy to not only part yourself from what you refer to as *the key*, but enough to regrow Yggdrasil."

"In other words, we need a lot of death," I clarified. I definitely wasn't sold on regrowing Yggdrasil, but parting myself from the key seemed like a good start regardless.

She nodded. "We'll need to move on from this place in the morning. Your enemies are near."

Well that was news.

"How close are they?" Alaric cut in, suddenly all business. "Have you seen them?"

The Morrigan's eyes flicked to Alaric, then back to me. Ignoring him while still answering his question, she said to me, "This corpse is not my only form," she gestured to her body, "and I saw much in my time away. Your enemies have left their holes to march forth. They search for *you* night and day, understanding the threat you pose. One still hopes to use you, while the other hopes to kill you, or so the rumors go amongst their troops."

I briefly wondered if it was Estus or Aislin that wanted to kill me, but really, it didn't matter. We couldn't wait around for either of them. We had to bring them together to fight each other, instead of us.

Echoing my thoughts, Alaric interjected, "We need to

make Estus believe Aislin is close to success in her endeavors. We must force him to act against her, rather than focusing his resources on finding Madeline."

The Morrigan finally acknowledged Alaric with a nod. "I do not think such a feat will be overly difficult. They are all afraid. The Vaettir's way of life will be changing no matter the outcome of this war. It puts doubt in the minds of the soldiers. A non-unified army is an easy target."

I yawned. Not that I wasn't interested in the Morrigan's plans, but the cold made me tired, and if we were leaving first thing in the morning, I would rather discuss the plans while we traveled.

Seeming to sense my need for rest, the Morrigan stood. "I would appreciate another moment alone before you retire."

I nodded and stood. Alaric didn't argue this time. If the Morrigan had wanted to harm me, she would have done so the first time we were alone.

I reached down and gave Alaric's arm a squeeze, then followed the Morrigan into the chilly darkness. I hoped this wouldn't be a long talk, as every moment spent away from the fire seemed to increase my fatigue.

Once we were out of sight in the darkness, the Morrigan stopped and leaned close to me conspiratorially. "How well do you know the child of Bastet?" she whispered, surprising me.

I narrowed my eyes suspiciously. "Well enough."

She sighed and linked my arm in hers. I tensed

initially, not liking the idea of buddying up with a goddess filled corpse. "In these matters, we must look out for ourselves. I need you to understand. He cannot comprehend the road before you, and will only cause you to fail."

I shook my head. "Alaric is one of the few reasons I'm still alive. He protects me."

The Morrigan smirked. "You are more than capable of protecting yourself. Your lack of belief in that point is part of the problem. You cannot rely on the help of others in this situation. You must find the strength within yourself."

My eyes narrowed even further, this time in suspicion. "But it's okay to accept *your* help?"

The Morrigan sighed, letting out a long stream of fog in the air. Whatever she'd done to the corpse she inhabited had given it true life, if it had the body heat and lung function for its breath to create fog.

"Accepting my help is different," she replied. "You must understand, I *am* you. We share the same energies. This has not occurred in a *very* long time. You're different from the Vaettir, *special*. I've waited for this day, but had begun to fear it would never come. I feared I was to remain one of a kind, and I was too weak to come back to this earth without aid. I explained to you that coming together with the key was fate. It was meant to be a part of you as much as anything else. You were brought into this world at this time on purpose."

I shook my head. None of what she was saying made

sense, or did it? "Say you're right," I began, "what does it change? I'm going to do my best to part myself with the key regardless of whether or not I'm fated to do so."

I hadn't expected the look of sympathy that crossed the Morrigan's face. "I must remember that you are still very young. You have not seen the world as I have, so I cannot expect you to view things clearly."

I frowned, feeling like I'd missed something. "If we're to leave first thing in the morning, we should get some rest."

The Morrigan nodded. "I do not require rest, but go if you must. Just remember what I told you."

I crossed my arms, *so* ready to go to bed, but needing to clarify something first. "I trust Alaric," I stated.

The Morrigan offered me a humoring smile. "Just see that your *trust* does not come back to bite you. A lady should not depend on anyone more than she depends on herself."

With that, she walked off into the darkness. I had no idea where she was planning on going, but I thought it best not to question her. I just had to trust she wouldn't run off and tell Estus or Aislin where we were.

I shook my head as I began walking back toward our camp. The Morrigan didn't want me to trust Alaric, yet expected me to blindly trust her. The thing about blind trust, is that it can only be given by fools. Trust is earned by actions, not words, and I knew exactly who had gained mine, and who hadn't.

❄

ALARIC SHOOK me awake early the next morning. I groaned as the warm sleeping bag was pulled down from my shoulders, exposing me to the harsh morning air.

He crouched and placed a light kiss on my cheek. "Everyone is ready to leave," he explained. "The Morrigan demanded that we let you sleep in."

I groaned and pushed the bedding the rest of the way down my body. The cold within the tent was a shock, but it was nothing compared to how it would be outside. I sat up and quickly slid myself into my coat, zipping it up to my neck, then searched around for my boots.

Alaric grabbed them from the other end of the tent, then handed them to me one by one.

"You should have argued with her," I groaned, irritated that everyone would now be waiting on me.

Not offended, Alaric smiled, then crouched down to kiss my slight baby bump through my coat. "Rest is important," he muttered.

I groaned again and moved away from him to begin lacing up my boots. I was not looking forward to the day's travels. The wind was incredibly cold with the speed of the snow mobiles, and the seats were hard and uncomfortable.

We hadn't discussed where we would go next, since Mikael and the others would have only learned we needed to leave that morning, presumably. Of course, they'd probably figured everything out while I was still in the tent, snoring away.

Alaric held open the tent door for me so I could struggle out into the blinding whiteness. You'd think sunny days would be welcome in such a cold area, but the glare on the surrounding white was a discomfort, even with sunglasses.

Mikael was suddenly there, offering me a hand up out of the tent. His long, auburn hair was once again loose in the cold air, but his reddish eyes were hidden behind a pair of expensive looking sunglasses. The sunglasses made me smile. He could feel human discomforts after all.

Alaric climbed out of the tent after me, his black stocking cap now on his head, but no sunglasses to be seen.

I looked past Mikael to the others. All the other tents had been packed up, and their previous occupants were now cooking breakfast around a small fire. I didn't see the Morrigan.

As if sensing my forthcoming question, Mikael explained, "She went to see how close we are to being discovered. We'll depart as soon as she returns."

He still held on to my hand. I looked down in question.

With an uneasy air, he gave my hand a squeeze. "I want you to be careful around her," he advised, referring to the Morrigan.

That I could sense his unease even around his shields meant he was very nervous indeed.

"I'm careful around everyone," I assured, half joking.

Alaric moved close to my side and Mikael's hand dropped.

Mikael's gaze moved to encompass both of us. "There are many myths surrounding the Morrigan," he explained. "She's more *human* than the other gods, if she's even a god at all. If the tales are true, she's driven by human emotions and motivations. We have no idea what her true agenda might be."

"So you not only tell lies, but you sense them too?" Alaric replied snarkily.

While the rivalry between Mikael and Alaric had temporarily lightened due to our present circumstances, they occasionally let everyone know it wasn't forgotten. It was irritating, but it was better than them trying to kill each other.

I didn't blame Alaric for wanting Mikael to pay for the death of his and Sophie's mother, but now really wasn't the time. I hoped *never* would be the time, since one of them would probably end up dead. I briefly wondered if Mikael would kill the father of my child, knowing what it would do to me. Of course, Alaric might not give him a choice. Then again, maybe Alaric would win.

I shivered. According to the Morrigan, I was stronger than I knew. Maybe I could stop them altogether. It would be worth a shot, given that I'd try regardless.

Ignoring Alaric's rude comment, Mikael angled his face to me to say something, then suddenly his lips shut tight as his shielded gaze looked past me.

I glanced over my shoulder to see the Morrigan approaching, still in the red-headed corpse. I really couldn't imagine her turning into a crow to scout for us, and wouldn't fully believe it until I saw it. Even with all that had happened, there were still some things I couldn't quite wrap my mind around.

"They are not far off," the Morrigan said as she closed the distance between us. She tossed her dark cloak back over her shoulder to reveal the plain black dress underneath. "But they approach on foot. We should be able to stay ahead of them. For now."

Mikael's tension kicked up a notch at the Morrigan's appearance, giving me the sensation of tiny ants crawling across my skin.

The Morrigan waited for my response, staring only at me, as if I was somehow in charge.

"Do we have time to eat?" I questioned.

I didn't like the idea of letting the other Vaettir gain on us any more than necessary, but my stomach was growling painfully, and it would be nearly impossible to eat while atop the snow mobiles.

The Morrigan nodded sharply, then led the way to the fire where James, Tabitha, Faas, Sophie, and Aila waited. I followed with Mikael and Alaric walking on either side of me.

Mikael leaned his 6'5" frame toward my shoulder. "Promise me?" he questioned.

I nodded. "I'll be careful," I whispered back.

Alaric took my gloved hand and gave it a squeeze. I had a thirteen-hundred year old Viking, and a five-hundred year old descendant of a war goddess to protect me. What could go wrong?

I shook my head at my own thoughts. The answer was *everything*. Like usual.

5

I had to admit, even with the discomfort, gliding across the ice on the snow mobiles was fun. I sat behind Alaric with my arms wrapped tightly around his waist. I watched the sparkling scenery drifting by until my nose was numb with cold, then ducked behind Alaric's broad shoulders to peer upward at a crow flying overhead.

My eyes narrowed into a glare as I watched the Morrigan's crow form drifting easily up and down on currents of chill air. I wouldn't have believed it was her if she hadn't changed right in front of us. The shift hadn't been the horrible limbs popping and cracking like in so many werewolf movies, rather, it was more like magic. The transformation only took seconds, and seemed painless. The result was a crow the size of a bald eagle, with gleaming black feathers slick as oil. Intelligence danced in those beady eyes, much more than was characteristic for the already intelligent species of bird.

I sighed and ducked my head back behind Alaric. If I was truly descended from the Morrigan, it would have been nice to inherit that bit of magic. Flying above everything where my enemies would never even recognize me was appealing . . . as long as I avoided any low-flying planes.

The machine beneath us slowed as the snow mobiles ahead of us came to a stop. I hoped it was lunchtime. We'd been riding for several hours. I'd grown hungry after one.

I swung my leg over the snow mobile, climbing down ahead of Alaric. I stretched my arms over my head, then flinched as a black shape swooped near. Just before hitting the ground, the Morrigan effortlessly transitioned back into human form, making me *more* than just a little jealous at how effortless the change was. Nothing was *that* effortless for me. Not even walking.

Sophie moved to stand at my side, glancing warily at the Morrigan. She tugged her black coat straight where it had bunched during her ride on the snowmobile, then leaned near my shoulder. "Are you absolutely sure she won't try to possess me again?"

I smirked. "Why don't you ask her?"

Sophie grumbled under her breath, dutifully ignoring the Morrigan's curious gaze.

Aila, who'd been riding with Sophie, joined us next. She seemed cranky, as usual, but didn't speak.

Finally Mikael joined us, glaring back at James. I refused the urge to smile patronizingly at them for being stuck together on the snow mobile when Sophie refused either of their company. Faas and Tabitha had ridden together, creepy siblings that they were.

Without a word, Mikael dug through a satchel slung across his shoulder, then began doling out protein bars. I took mine with a frown, then glared down at the brightly colored packaging. While we'd cooked much of our food during our time at camp, the protein bars had been our extra ration. They were thick, hard to chew, and tasted *delightfully* like wet cardboard.

I started to open the bar, then jumped when I realized the Morrigan was standing right beside me. "A moment, please?" she questioned.

I lowered the bar to my side. I was getting tired of these *moments*. Interacting with the Morrigan at all was unnerving, and speaking alone with her increased that anxiety tenfold. Of course, since we needed her help, I couldn't exactly say no. We had, after all, summoned her to us, and not the other way around.

I nodded, but Mikael caught my eye before we could walk away. His look said it all, *be careful*. Alaric watched me with much the same look, except with the added effect of biting his lip to keep himself from speaking. I could sense how much it cost him to hold himself back as I turned away with the Morrigan at my side.

Uncomfortable with everyone's worried gazes on my back, I followed the Morrigan out into the crisp white expanse. The stiffness slowly left my legs as we walked, and I grew more comfortable with every crunching step.

I looked at our feet as I realized I couldn't even hear the Morrigan's boots on the snow. My own gait in my heavy snow boots made an annoying *crunch* with every step, while she glided along like a dainty ballerina.

My shoulders slumped. *Someday* I'd meet another clumsy supernatural being. There *had* to be another one out there.

Unsure of how far we were going to walk, I unwrapped my protein bar and took a bite. I wasn't about to miss my only chance at sustenance.

My bar was half gone by the time she finally turned to me. I glanced back, even though I knew the others would be out of sight. Suddenly I felt nervous, Mikael's words echoing in my mind.

"We probably shouldn't be out here much longer," I said weakly, fiddling with the half-eaten bar in my gloved hands. "We want to be far away from our last camp before we end our travels for the night."

The Morrigan's dark eyes peered into mine for several seconds, then she held out her hand. "Take my hand, please," she instructed. "I will not harm you."

My instincts screamed at me to run. I took a step back instead. "Why do I feel like your version of harm is different from mine?"

She frowned, her hand still outstretched. "I'm here to *help* you. I would not do anything to keep my sole descendant from greatness."

I did *not* like the way she'd said *greatness*. I didn't want any greatness, period. I just wanted to stay, you know … alive.

I lifted my foot to take another step back, then stumbled as she lunged forward, latching on to my hand.

"Hey!" someone shouted.

We both turned.

James ran toward us. "Let her go!"

Even though he was *James*, he looked for the life of me like a angel in that moment.

"Why did you follow us?" the Morrigan snapped, dropping my hand.

James looked smug as he reached us. "Everyone can keep me in the dark all they want. I'm not helpless, and I can find out information on my own."

"So you came to *spy*?" the Morrigan hissed.

I sighed. James wasn't a very good spy if he revealed himself at the first sign of trouble, not that I wasn't grateful for the interruption.

My gratitude came to a screeching halt as the Morrigan waved a hand in front of James' face, and he instantly dropped to the ground.

My jaw wide open, I looked from James' prostrate form, then back to the Morrigan. Before I could react, she grabbed my hand again. I tugged against her grip, but my limbs felt incredibly weak, then I couldn't feel anything at all.

My vision shifted like I was falling forward, but instead of hitting the ground, I was being pulled away from it. I watched the ground in horror as I rose higher and higher. I could see black wings in my peripheral vision, moving up and down as I gained altitude.

Though I could feel little else, I felt it as my heart sank down in realization. I was part of a crow, but I had no control. The Morrigan was steering. I was just an unwilling passenger along for the ride.

I screamed in my mind, but had no mouth to actually express it. She was taking me away from Alaric, and Mikael, and *everyone*, yet all I could think about was my baby. If I was no longer in my natural form, where had my baby gone? Could it be a part of the bird too? I cried with no eyes to shed tears as the Morrigan carried me farther away from everything I held dear.

"THEY'VE BEEN GONE for far too long," Alaric announced, restless for Madeline's return. He knew he never should have let Madeline walk off with the Morrigan to begin with. They'd done it twice before, but each time was still a risk, a risk he was a fool to take.

Mikael nodded, peering in the direction Madeline had gone. "Agreed."

Alaric hated that he and the Viking were agreeing on most things lately, but he could swallow his pride for now if it meant helping Madeline. He internally chastised himself again for letting her go. He'd convinced himself it was safe, but now they hadn't returned, and he couldn't argue with the sick feeling in his gut.

"Let's go," Mikael ordered, needing no further prompting.

Alaric did not appreciate how much Mikael had grown to care for Madeline, but if it meant extra protection for her, well, he could bear that too. For now. Madeline needed all the allies she could get.

Scenting the air for Maddy, Alaric hurried across the snow with Mikael at his side. Footsteps trotted up behind them, then Sophie was at his other side. The others stayed with the snow mobiles, not that there was anyone around the barren, frozen wasteland to steal them.

The snowy ground was hard packed enough that footprints were barely visible, but Alaric could smell where Madeline had walked. Her smell had become more familiar to him than any other, save that of his sister.

Sophie inhaled deeply through her nose. "Did anyone notice where James went? His scent is in this direction."

"He claimed he was going for a short walk," Mikael replied. "I thought little of it."

Alaric's eyes narrowed. There was little doubting by this point that James' memory was truly lost, it was no act, but what if it had suddenly returned to him? Would he try to harm or kidnap Madeline?

He walked faster, then picked up speed to run.

Mikael and Sophie both kept pace with him easily. Something was very wrong. He shouldn't have let Madeline walk off without him.

A crumpled form came into view, but it was too big to be Madeline. *James*. Alaric looked down as he reached him. He was clearly still alive, but unconscious. Beside him was a half-eaten protein bar. Alaric picked it up and could smell Madeline all over it, yet her scent ended there. It did not lead off into any other direction.

At first, he couldn't help but look around their snowy surroundings for some other clue, then he thought of the Morrigan's crow form, and how easily she shifted. Protcin bar still gripped in his hand, he looked up at the sky as the pieces fell into place.

IT SEEMED like we had flown for days, with me silently screaming all the while. The Morrigan never seemed to tire. We'd flown over the ocean, across an expanse of land, then another large expanse of water. Eventually a green, rocky coastline came into view. We continued onward, then began to lose altitude over a circular, rocky outcropping.

The moment we touched down, we separated. I fell to the loamy earth coughing and gasping for breath, shocked to have my body back.

"My baby!" I croaked, cradling my stomach.

The Morrigan looked down at me, her red hair whipping about in the wind. "The child is fine, though you could have told me of her presence sooner. It was quite a shock to realize we had an extra passenger."

Tears flowed down my face, as hard as I fought them. "I wasn't planning on being turned into a bird!" I shouted. Then it clicked what the Morrigan had just said. "Her?" I questioned weakly.

A small smile played across her face, but instead of answering me, she ordered, "Get to your feet. I'm tired from our journey, and desire shelter. Listening to you scream for such a long distance has given me a headache."

I stayed right where I was sitting, the damp grass unable to penetrate my black ski pants. "Take me back to Alaric," I demanded.

She shook her head. "It was too risky to remain with your companions. They would only slow you down. We're better off on our own."

"No," I argued. "We have to go back. We can at least bring them here."

The Morrigan smirked. "I would not share such an experience with any of them, even if I could, but it doesn't matter, because I cannot. I was only able to change your form because it is a gift you would have had if you were stronger."

I frowned, still holding a hand to my tummy to reassure myself that the baby was really still there. The idea of having such an amazing gift was appealing, but not if it would make me any more like the Morrigan than I already was.

"I will not take you back," she continued, "so your choices are to sit here in the grass and starve, or to come with me and take care of your child."

My frown deepened. She had a point. I didn't know where I was, but there were no signs of civilization. Who knew how far the nearest town might be? I would need to get my bearings, and hopefully some supplies, before I tried to escape.

My heart felt hollow as I realized that even if I escaped, I would have no way of finding Alaric and the others. They were in hiding, after all. My greatest hope was the small chance that the Morrigan might take me back to them.

She turned and walked away from me as I scrambled to my feet. Now that I was standing, I could see large jagged rocks spanning for miles, all covered in green moss and surrounded by lush grass. The air was chilly, but not as cold as where we'd been.

I followed the Morrigan as she led the way toward the circle of rocks I'd noticed from the air. Each of them was larger than a person, and they formed a perfect half-circle, almost as if they'd been placed there on purpose.

The Morrigan moved to the center of the circle, then crouched down to retrieve something from the ground. She came up with a stone in each hand, offering one to me as I reached her. Curiosity got the better of me, and I took the offered stone.

A moment later, I felt a strange sinking feeling, as if we'd stepped into quicksand. I panicked and tried to step away, but I was too late. We sunk into the earth, then came out the other side.

I gasped, crouching where I had landed as the space we were now in slowly illuminated. Familiar stone walls met my eyes.

"A Salr?" I questioned, slowly rising. "How did you bring us here? I thought only the Vaettir could find them."

The Morrigan smirked. "You really are an arrogant race. Who do you think *created* the Salr?"

I gave her a shocked look. Surely she couldn't mean—

She rolled her eyes. "No, not me, you silly thing, but the magic of the old gods. These sanctuaries were the last gift to their children before Yggdrasil was destroyed."

Her explanation made me more confused, not less. "I thought we were more like the Norns' children, not the gods'."

The Morrigan brushed off her cloak, though I could see no dirt on it, then walked past me, further into the Salr. "Many of you were made in the gods' images, and they loved you just as the Norns did. Then you destroyed Yggdrasil, and cast the Norns out to die."

I hurried to catch up. "Sorry?" I offered, even though I hadn't been alive when everything she'd recounted took place.

"Hrmf," was the Morrigan's only reply. She led us

down a narrow, stone hall, trailing her fingertips across the stones as we walked.

I glanced around warily, ready for a Norn to pop out at any moment. "I notice you didn't include yourself when you were speaking about the gods. You said *they* not *we*."

"We are the same, and we are different," she replied.

I let out a long, frustrated sigh, not understanding, but sensing that I wouldn't be receiving any real explanation.

"How long are we staying here?" I grumbled.

"Long enough to prepare," she answered vaguely.

I stopped walking. "Prepare for what?"

She continued walking, forcing me to either catch up to her, or remain alone in the hall. I caught up.

"For war," she answered as soon as I reached her side.

I huffed. "I thought that's what we were already doing."

The Morrigan stopped walking and turned to fully face me with a stern expression, making me half-regret even speaking to begin with.

"My dear child," she said in a lecturing tone, "we can talk strategy until we all turn to dust. There is still one simple fact that cannot be ignored."

"And what is that?" I asked snidely, crossing my arms.

A small smile curled her lips. "For war you need an army," she replied. "And I'm going to help you build one."

I opened my mouth, then closed it, unsure of what to say. An army didn't sound like a terrible thing, depending on the soldiers. An army could protect us. It could keep Alaric and Mikael out of the fighting altogether. An army could also turn on us and send us all to our graves, but there was no use dwelling on *ifs* in dire times such as these.

"So you agree?" she pressed, watching my expression as I muddled over what she'd said.

I shrugged, feeling sick and wanting nothing more than to lie down. "Do I have a choice?"

She grinned. "There is always a choice, Madeline. I'm here to show you that."

She turned and continued walking before I could argue that she was showing me quite the opposite.

6

James sat on the ice, glaring at everyone. Alaric and Mikael had dragged him back to camp while Sophie walked ahead, refusing to help. James had woken eventually. Alaric had expected him to be whiney and frightened, but he'd been in for quite the suprise.

"What happened to Madeline?" Alaric demanded, barely restraining himself from throttling the man at his feet.

James smiled coldly, a smile that was all old James, not the James without his memory. "I'll answer your questions when you answer mine."

James was outnumbered, surrounded by Alaric, Sophie, and Mikael and his people, yet he wouldn't tell them a damn thing. He sat smugly on the ice, warm and comfortable within his snow gear.

"I don't know what happened to Diana," Alaric lied for the fifth time.

If James found out Madeline had killed his grand-mother, he'd likely not be inclined to help rescue her. Of course, now that James was back to his old self, he likely wouldn't be inclined to help either way.

"You're lying," James said simply.

Mikael grunted. "We could just torture him," he suggested.

Alaric shook his head. "It won't do any good."

He knew James better than that. They could cut off his fingers and toes one by one, and he wouldn't say a word. He turned back to James, his shoulders slumped in resignation. Nope, he wouldn't tell them a damn thing until his questions were answered.

"Diana is dead," Alaric explained. "She forced Madeline's hand, and Madeline killed her."

James surprised Alaric by smiling, then surprised him even more by erupting with laughter. "Little mouse has teeth after all," he mused.

Mikael let out a long whistle. "Not the reaction I was expecting."

Besides Sophie and Madeline, Mikael had been the only other who knew the truth about Diana. Maddy hadn't even wanted to admit to herself that she'd raised several corpses to tear Diana to pieces, all before the Norn cut out her heart to release the key. Aila's confused expression confirmed that Mikael had kept his mouth shut on all he'd been told.

"Diana was a tool to be used like any other," James explained.

Sophie huffed. "Do you truly care about no one?"

James glared at her. "Diana left me to be arrested back at the hotel, so she could escape and follow Madeline. Had I been killed, she would not have shed a tear. I owe her no loyalty."

Well that was good news, Alaric thought. Though he despised James, he might still prove useful. "Now tell us what happened," he demanded.

James smiled up at him. "*Fine.* I had followed Madeline and the Morrigan, not trusting the Morrigan's intentions. I tried to interject when the Morrigan grabbed Madeline. Then the witch waved her hand and I was out like a light. When I woke up, I remembered everything. Everything from before, and everything since." His expression turned bitter at that, obviously displeased with the events after his memory loss.

Alaric smiled coldly. He sincerely hoped that was the case, and that James remembered acting like a scared little child. Judging by James' glare, he did. Alaric smiled wider.

"That tells us nothing," Mikael cut in. "How do we find her?"

James smirked up at him. "Why do you care, *Viking*?"

Mikael growled and lunged at James, but Aila darted in to hold him back. Seeming to regain his composure, Mikael straightened.

"Madeline and I have a blood oath," he said simply. "I must at least try to find her."

Alaric doubted that was the real reason, but said

nothing to that effect. Arguing with Mikael would do no good, though it was hard to tell that to the burning ball of rage and jealousy in his gut.

Pushing back his emotions, he turned back to James. "You know we cannot let you go."

James laughed. "And I don't plan on leaving. I want to be on the team with the big scary charm and the evil witch."

"You would abandon Aislin, just like that?" Alaric questioned.

James rose to his feet, and no one stopped him. "I remained at Estus' side for thirty years on Aislin's orders, and look where that's gotten me. I was without my memory for weeks, and the people who took care of me were those I might consider enemies, not those I've sworn loyalty to. No, I'll take my chances with team wild card."

Sophie finally stepped forward. "What if we don't want you?"

James took a step toward Sophie, putting himself inches from her face. "If you didn't want me, then I wouldn't be here," he teased with an infuriating smile.

With a growl Sophie turned on her heel, then stalked off across the ice. Alaric shook his head, he would much rather kill James than bring him along, but he had an idea growing in his mind. One where James, now that he was James again, might prove very useful indeed.

"Pack everything up," Alaric ordered. "We need to get moving as soon as Sophie finishes her tantrum."

Mikael had turned to gaze off into the distance, keeping his thoughts on everything to himself. It was one of those moments where Alaric wished he had Madeline's unusual abilities. He would have very much liked to know what the Viking was thinking and feeling right at that time.

Not that Alaric cared about Mikael's emotions, but the game they played had just been irreparably altered. Alaric would not lose to the Morrigan, and he would not lose to Mikael. The prize for winning was simple. He would keep Madeline and his child safe. It was a prize worth more than any amount of riches.

AFTER WE'D SETTLED into the Salr, the Morrigan had provided food and clothing more suited to our current environment. I had no idea where she'd gotten any of it, but I grudgingly appreciated that she'd actually taken into account my vegetarian sensibilities. The clothes weren't bad either. The gray jeans fit comfortably, as did the forest green, chunky knit sweater. The brown leather boots weren't what I would have chosen, but that was about it. I'd been able to take a hot bath, which was a huge luxury after my time spent in the icy wilds. I wasn't able to enjoy it like I would have if I knew everyone else was safe, but I hadn't turned my nose up at it either.

Besides the painful ball of worry in my gut, the only other thing wrong with the situation was the company.

The Morrigan sat across from me at a large, plain wood table, ignoring me. She poured over an ancient looking book that had left a rectangle of dust on the table, while I gnawed at the remainder of my apple core and watched her every move.

My thoughts turned back to Alaric. Was he safe? Had our small party been found by our *enemies*, or had the Morrigan made the entire thing up? Would he and Sophie remain with Mikael's people, now that I'd disappeared, along with the charm that their plans relied on?

I shivered. I knew Alaric would look for me, but there was no way he'd be able to find me. It would be up to me to get back to him.

Looking up from her book to notice my shiver, the Morrigan waved her hand at the small fire in the stone fireplace, making the flames roar at full steam. She was gladly accommodating all of my needs, yet my pleas to take me back to my companions had fallen on deaf ears.

"What are you reading?" I asked, unable to sit in silence any longer. I grabbed the ends of my now-clean hair and pawed at them nervously.

"Rituals," she muttered absently. "We'll need to brush up to make sure we get everything right."

"What sort of rituals?" I pressed.

She slammed the book shut suddenly and gave me her full attention. "What do you know of the legends concerning me?" she questioned abruptly.

"N-not much," I muttered, taken aback by the sudden attention.

She laughed bitterly. "Of course you don't. I'm sure if I asked you about Odin or Ra, you'd sing a different tune."

Not knowing what to say, I said nothing.

She sighed. "Many legends refer to me as the *Phantom Queen*. In many regards, they are right. It was not always so, but near the end of my time in these lands, I had the need for an army. I called to my side the banshees and other phantoms."

Just from what I'd learned of the Morrigan in the short time since I'd met her, I couldn't help but believe everything she was saying. She *seemed* just like a banshee queen.

"If things go according to my plans, you will have the power you need to rid yourself of the foreign energy inside you," she continued. "And our army shall protect you while your enemies are slain."

I shivered. This was the plan *I* had set into motion. I couldn't really pretend to be morally above it now.

"I have a question," I interjected, trying my best to ignore all of the bloody implications in favor of a question that had been vexing me.

She nodded. "Go on."

I bit my lip, not sure how to phrase what I wanted to know. Best to start from the beginning. "Several weeks before we summoned you, the key had taken me over. It kind of *possessed* me. When the others tried to remove it from my neck, it absorbed into my body. Long story short, I ended up meeting with one of the Norns. She conveyed that I could either die, thus taking the key with me, or I could put its energy into my child, thus giving the key human form. I rejected either option."

The Morrigan leaned forward over her old book, listening intently.

"The key has been dormant since then," I continued. "I felt it for a moment when you were summoned, but that's it. I'm frightened, because when I learned to shield myself from it, it learned the same. I feel like it's plotting something, but I have no way of telling."

She stood abruptly and walked around the table. I tensed as she moved behind me, then jumped as her hands landed gently on my shoulders.

She was silent for several heartbeats, then removed her hands. "I can sense its presence," she remarked as she moved around the table to reclaim her seat, "but little else. It is shielding very tightly."

"You're an empath too?" I asked breathlessly.

The Morrigan rolled her eyes. "As I said, you and I are the same. Any gifts you have are mine."

I let out a shaky sigh. The fire was making it too warm in the room, and I desperately wanted some fresh air.

"What about what the Norn said?" I forced myself to ask. "She claimed the only way for me to be rid of the key at this point was through death, or through my child."

The Morrigan smirked. "She was speaking in effect

to who you were *then*, not to who you have the potential to become. Fate is a tricky thing. Her answer was in response to available solutions in that very moment, based on the person you were, and decisions you were capable of making."

My face fell in confusion. As far as I knew, I'd always been the same person, and always would be.

She tsked at me. "You are weak, Madeline. You look to others to save you. You do not have the will to force the key out of you. You barely have the will to block it out of your thoughts. This weakness has shaped who you are, but it is also a choice."

My face burned with a blush. "I'm not weak," I argued. "You have no idea what I've been through."

"Those are the words of a child," the Morrigan snapped, then said sarcastically, "Poor me, I've fought so hard." Her eyes hardened. "None of it matters. What matters is the person you are today. When there is danger, you look first to others for protection. When there are decisions, you yield to others, believing your opinions are invalid. *You* are *weak*."

"Fine!" I shouted, just wanting her to shut up. "If I'm so weak, then why even waste your time on me? If I'm bound to fail, then why even try?"

Her stern expression suddenly transitioned to a sympathetic smile as her eyes went somewhat distant. "I was weak once too," she mused.

"What changed?" I asked shakily.

Her eyes met mine. "I was forced to stand on my own. The only way to break the cycle of depending on others is to stand on your own, *really* on your own. The only way you can become the person you need to be to control the power inside you, is to make the choice to do it yourself."

A few wretched tears slipped out. "That's why you took me away from the others," I accused. "It wasn't because they were slowing us down."

"They were slowing *you* down," she replied. "Holding you back."

I shook my head. "I wouldn't be alive if not for Alaric."

"Wouldn't you?" she questioned seriously. "Tell me, I've only been with you a short time, so tell me when he's saved you."

I thought about it. I'd escaped Estus' Salr with the help of James. I'd defeated Diana with my magic. We'd travelled back to the present time with energy I'd stolen from Yggdrasil.

"When we were attacked in Estus' Salr," I blurted, trying to recall the exact event. All of the emergencies had somewhat blurred together in my mind. "One of Aislin's people had spotted me, and was coming toward me with an intent to harm. Alaric killed him."

"But this harmful man, he never actually reached you?" the Morrigan said as if she already knew the answer.

I frowned.

"How do you know you would not have saved yourself, had Alaric not been present? How do you know that if he had been somewhere else, that you wouldn't be alive today?"

My frown deepened. I didn't.

"Now tell me of the times you have saved yourself," she instructed.

I went back over everything I'd just gone through in my head, but didn't say any of it out loud.

Still, the Morrigan smiled, satisfied. "The truth is, though you've had help, you have no proof you couldn't have done all of it on your own. You feel you need a protector, without realizing you already have one inside you."

I went silent. I couldn't really argue, but I didn't exactly agree with her either. There might have been no proof I *couldn't* have done it all on my own, but there was also no proof that I could.

Really not wanting to discuss things further, I stood. "I'm going to take a look around," I announced, hoping she'd actually let me.

She nodded. "Think on what I've said."

I nodded quickly and hurried for the door.

"And Madeline?" she questioned, halting me mid-motion. "I've sealed all entrances to this Salr. Don't waste your time trying to escape me."

I gritted my teeth and finished my advance toward

the door. For someone who wanted me to stand on my own two feet, she sure was treating me like a child.

I let myself out into the hall and shut the door behind me. As soon as I was alone, I breathed a sigh of relief. I might not be able to leave, but it was nice to be away from the Morrigan's overwhelming presence.

I walked back toward the entrance we'd come through, unable to simply trust it was actually sealed. I at least had to *try*.

Sure enough, once I was in the entry room, there was no apparent way out. I touched the walls, and even used a rickety chair so I could touch the ceiling. There was no feel of magic to any of it.

Resigned, I journeyed back into the long hallway, not really paying attention to where I was going. I went through several twists and turns, occasionally checking behind closed doors, only to find barren rooms. I was just about to turn around and go back to find the Morrigan to ask her where I was supposed to sleep, when a noise caught my attention.

It sounded like a *psst*, followed by a giggle. More curious than I was afraid, I looked to my left. There was a door, slightly ajar. I'd ignored it since all the other rooms had been empty.

A small voice whispered, "Hey!"

My heart gave a little jump as I took a step closer and peered into the darkness seeping around the edges of the door. The rough wood slowly opened a little further inward, as if beckoning me inside.

Steeling myself for an attack, I pushed the door the rest of the way inward. The room within gradually lit of its own accord to reveal what was either a tiny woman or a child. It was hard to tell which. Her hair was dark green, but it was a green that looked natural, not dyed. It had highlights right where the sun would hit, and other subtle variations in color throughout. Rough-cut bangs obscured the upper portion of her face, which was delicate and angular, boasting large, sparkly hazel eyes that gave her a childlike appearance, though upon closer observation, I was pretty sure she was an adult.

Still, she couldn't have been more than five feet tall. Her clothes were a mishmash of different fabrics and styles, pairing a loose, long skirt with a button up tank top, and a pastel pink cardigan that clashed with the more vivid colors of her other clothing.

She gestured frantically with a tiny hand for me to step into the room, which I did without thinking. The door shut of its own accord behind me.

The room was clearly the small woman's living quarters, which meant she was likely Vaettir, if she was able to get inside to begin with. Her bed was made of straw, and the room was dotted with various crystals, shells, and other things that could be collected outside.

"What are you doing here?" she whispered. "No one has come to this place in a very long time."

"Who are you?" I whispered back, still feeling wary.

She looked slightly startled by the question. "I'm Kira," she answered, pointing at her chest.

"Are you Vaettir?" I asked, wondering just how long she'd been in the Salr alone.

"I know that word," she said thoughtfully.

I nodded. "I'm Vaettir too. How long have you been here alone?"

She shrugged. "I'm not sure, but I'm not alone. The humans up above think I'm a fairy. They give me clothes and food, and they don't tell anyone about me."

My eyes widened. She'd somehow been living on her own and interacting with humans, while remaining off the radar of the other Vaettir.

"How on earth have you managed to live this way?" I marveled.

Misinterpreting my question, she answered. "The humans enjoy my gifts. I can make the flowers grow, and I watch over their gardens."

I shook my head. "I mean, how have you remained hidden from other Vaettir? We're not allowed to interact with humans any more than necessary."

Kira's eyes widened. "I didn't know! I'm good at hiding. I can hide from the humans too if that's what I'm supposed to do."

At the third mention of the humans, it finally clicked. Kira knew the way to civilization, and she knew the way in and out of the Salr.

She watched me silently as I thought things over, clearly panicked.

"I'm sorry," I blurted, realizing that she was waiting for me to explain things to her. "If you've remained hidden from the Vaettir this long, you probably don't need to hide from your human friends."

Kira heaved a sigh of relief, then asked, "Why are you with the Morrigan? I thought she left us long ago."

I inhaled sharply. "How do you know who she is?"

Kira seemed confused. "I remember her, somehow, from a very long time ago."

Woah. If Kira had seen the Morrigan before, that meant she was very, *very* old. Then something hit me that didn't quite make sense. "The Morrigan hasn't always looked like she does now. How did you recognize her?"

Kira's eyes widened. "Can you not feel her power? She's sealed us within the Salr with only a thought."

My hope deflated. If Kira was stuck here too, she couldn't show me the way out. "It won't be permanent," I soothed. "We're only staying here for a little while."

I didn't feel the need to mention we'd be using the Salr as a sanctuary while we summoned a dark army of phantoms.

Kira suddenly looked worried again. "Just be sure to do what she says while you're here," she warned. "You don't want to end up like Cúchulainn."

"Cúchulaiin?" I questioned, not having heard the name before.

Kira nodded and looked toward the door as if afraid the Morrigan would come bursting in at any moment. She turned back to me. "The Morrigan's only love. He seduced her, wanting her support in battle. She was once

79

known as a great champion of warriors, protecting them in their endeavors. He eventually grew vain, and cast her aside, thinking he was powerful enough to make his conquests on his own. Outraged, the Morrigan hindered him in battle from that point forth. She could have killed him initially, but wanted his humiliation first. When he was finally slain, she appeared as a crow on his shoulder, showing him the darkness she would inflict upon his soul, even after death. She left this world shortly after. Many say she followed him into the underworld to torment him even there."

I shivered. I could see the Morrigan doing just as Kira claimed, and it explained her distaste for men.

"You should probably stay hidden," I advised, starting to worry that the Morrigan would come looking for me soon. "I'll come speak with you again, if I can."

Kira nodded as I turned to go.

"Hey!" she whispered before I could push the door open. "What's your name?"

I turned back to look at her. "Madeline," I answered, "but you can call me Maddy."

Kira nodded and smiled. "I can feel your power too, Maddy. Don't let the Morrigan change who you are."

With that unsettling warning, I nodded and turned to go. The Morrigan had said she wanted to make me strong. With the new information from Kira, I couldn't help but wonder just what that might entail.

On one hand, strength in times of conflict was necessary, but at what cost? Was it strong to sacrifice few for the good of many? Was it strong to risk summoning an army of spirits to save yourself and your child? I knew there were many differences, but at that moment, as I crept back down the hallway, strength and selfishness seemed to go hand in hand.

7

Alaric glanced at James, creeping along silently in the darkness beside him toward the Salr. He felt uneasy with only James at his side, and even more uneasy with the plan in general.

Mikael was the one most skilled at negotiations, but he'd remained behind with the others. If things did not go as planned, *someone* would still need to save Madeline. Alaric hated the fact that it would have to be Mikael, but the Viking also stood the greatest chance of accomplishing the task, should Alaric perish.

He trusted Sophie to rescue Madeline too, but she wasn't as strong as Mikael, nor did she have the support of a clan. Mikael might have had many faults, but Alaric could almost guarantee he would protect Madeline, even though she carried Alaric's unborn child.

James gestured in the darkness, pointing toward the entrance. Alaric's eyes followed to where he pointed.

A large tree stump stood forlornly amidst the other trees, emitting a faint, familiar magic. He could only hope that past that entrance, would be Aislin. Since she had become Doyen for several clans, she had Salr in different countries, including this one in Norway. As Aislin's spy, James had known the location, though he couldn't guarantee Aislin would actually be there. Regardless, even if she was not somewhere below them, they might at least succeed in getting a message to her. A message filled with half-truths that might trick her into helping them, at least for the time being.

She didn't need to know James had turned on her, or that Alaric would sooner die than to give her Maddy. All Aislin needed to know was that Madeline had been kidnapped, and Alaric was desperate to find her. Desperate enough to join Aislin's clan, and to help her control Madeline. Hopefully the lie, being so bold and backed by his love for Madeline, would persuade Aislin to believe it.

The Norns' slaughter caused him to believe Aislin had a way of tracking Madeline, or perhaps of tracking them all, since she'd found them so easily. Then again, maybe she had just tracked the key. It made no difference as long as she could find Madeline or the key again.

Without tracking them, finding the Norn's Salr would have been near impossible. An idea supported by the fact that Mikael had kept it hidden for centuries. Aislin *had* to have a way to find Madeline for any of it to be possible.

James ran his hand over the surface of the tree stump. Moments later, a staircase appeared, level with the earth, leading downward. James went first. Alaric followed, relieved to not have the treacherous man at his back. Of course, Alaric supposed he was a treacherous man himself, shirking all former allegiances in the name of love. Estus had not been the first Doyen he'd served, but he would be the last, despite any consequences. He would never again stand by while someone he loved was tortured.

It *was* love, this thing he felt for Madeline. He wasn't sure if his draw to her was due to their similar natures, or to the fact that she was so different than other Vaettir. Either way, he was willing to die for her, a point he might well prove in the next few minutes.

Heading down the spiraling staircase, he found a Salr that looked much like any other. Nearing the bottom, two women came into view, clearly on guard duty judging by their stance, leather armor, and cold stares leveled at James and Alaric as they descended the stairs. Just one step above them, James halted. Alaric's stomach twisted as the ruse was about to begin.

One woman was small, with short gray hair, while the other was tall, with blonde hair cropped close to her head.

The gray haired woman smirked. "We never thought to see *you* again," she said to James. "Aislin will be pleased you yet live."

James nodded curtly. "Is she here?"

85

The blonde woman answered, "She is, but she grants audiences to very few."

"Trust me, she's going to want to hear what we have to say."

The older-looking woman smiled softly. "We shall see."

She turned and led the way deeper into the Salr, leaving the blonde woman behind to keep guard.

As James and Alaric followed, the blonde guard watched them warily. She was nervous about something, though whether it was due to Alaric's and James' presence, or something else, he did not know.

They left the entry room and continued walking. Other Vaettir watched as they passed by in the halls. Some nodded in recognition of James, but none spoke. Alaric did his best to quell his anxiety. There was no telling who else might have the gift of empathy, like Madeline, and he didn't want to give away any more information than necessary.

Eventually they reached a heavy wooden door with two more guards outside, one male and one female, both wearing the same leather armor as the stair guards.

The woman guard leaned against the wall casually, her long, red hair trailing across the stone, while the man stood at attention. Everything about him said *military*, from his crew-cut black hair to his ramrod straight spine, though he'd likely never been enlisted.

Vaettir were prohibited from joining human organizations unless it was to the direct benefit of the Vaettir, like in the case of police or social workers. Having a single soldier in the military wouldn't do any good, unless Aislin was gathering information. The thought made Alaric's stomach flip flop nervously.

Their escort looked the red haired woman up and down with distaste, then turned her attention to the male guard. "Tell the Doyen her spy is here, and that he is accompanied by . . . " She turned to Alaric.

"Alaric," he answered, assuming that with Aislin's intel, she would recognize his name.

The male guard turned and opened the door just enough to quickly slip into the room, careful to not let Alaric or James see inside.

Several painful moments later, he returned, opening the door fully. "She'll see you."

With a smug expression, James led the way inside. Alaric nodded to their chaperone and the red-haired guard, then followed.

The contrast between the room they entered compared to the rest of the Salr was jarring. Vintage lace and pastel velvet covered everything. The room edged on Victorian, but with hints of medieval, like the heavy wooden table where Aislin sat, pushed off to one side.

Ignoring them, Aislin lifted a spoon to her thin lips, calmly eating her supper despite the appearance of her visitors. Alaric's eyes narrowed as he scrutinized her. She wore a dressing gown that would have seemed casual, if not for the tiny gemstones sewn into the fabric. Her gray hair was curled into an ornate updo, topped by a simple tiara. Several attendants in leather armor surrounded her.

Aislin ate a final spoonful of her soup, set down her utensil, then dabbed her lips delicately with a cream colored napkin. With a regal air, she gestured for one of the attendants to remove her bowl. Once the attendant with the bowl silently let himself out of the room, Aislin stood.

"I thought perhaps you'd betrayed me," she said calmly to James, her lined face dispassionate.

"I was temporarily without my memory due to a blow on the head," he explained. "I only just recently regained knowledge of the past thirty years or so."

Aislin's lips sealed into a tight line. "You were there that night, the night Madeline used the charm to defeat my executioner. You fought for the wrong side."

If James was nervous, he didn't show it. "As I explained, I had lost my memory. Now that I have regained it, my allegiance is with you."

Aislin cocked her head in apparent deep thought. Alaric kept his breathing even, his stance relaxed, though he was quite sure he and James were about to die.

With a surprising nod of assent, Aislin turned her pale eyes to Alaric. "You were there that night as well, you stood at Madeline's side. I cannot believe that *you* have suddenly decided to choose the correct side."

Alaric glanced at James, then spoke. "Madeline and I had hoped to use the charm as a bargaining tool to join your clan, as we desired protection from Estus. Siding with Mikael's people was a temporary allegiance, at best."

"Ah Mikael," Aislin mused. "How I would like to get my hands on him. Where is our Viking friend?"

Alaric didn't have to fake his frown in regards to Mikael. "We parted ways when Madeline was kidnapped. He did not view rescuing her as a feasible option."

Aislin laughed. "Now it all becomes clear. You hope I can find the girl, but why would I want to do such a thing?"

Alaric smiled. "Because you want to find the charm before Estus."

Aislin shrugged. "I spent centuries searching for the charm, until one of the Norns informed me that an executioner would use the dead to find it. Part of that information was relayed to Estus, unfortunately, setting this competition into motion."

"You speak to the Norns?" Alaric asked, truly astonished. Until recently, most Vaettir, except Mikael, had been under the impression the Norns no longer existed, and perhaps they never had.

Aislin fluttered her lashes, clearly bored. "That's besides the point. My point, is that I have waited for the charm for centuries, and I will wait centuries more if need be. Long enough for Madeline to perish, and for the charm to become fully available to *me*."

Alaric doubted Aislin had several more centuries in

her. She'd aged a great deal over her long life, unlike him or Mikael. Her powers might be frightening, but she wasn't powerful enough to live forever. Still, it would likely be a moot point to argue with her, especially when he had valuable information to spur her into action.

"The charm has left behind its physical form," he explained. "It now dwells within Madeline. When she dies, its energy will be released back into the universe. Whatever it is you intend to accomplish, it will have to be soon."

Aislin growled and slammed her dainty fist down onto the table, then turned ire-filled eyes to James. "Is this true?" she demanded.

James nodded. "I retained my memories during my lost time. I saw the charm withdraw into her body myself."

Aislin gritted her teeth. "I will kill the girl before I let her use the charm against me."

Panic washed through him. He debated killing Aislin then and there, heedless of her guards, but instead raised a finger into the air. "There is another way," he suggested, giving everything he had into keeping his voice calm.

"And *what* is that?" Aislin snapped.

Alaric took a step toward the terrifying little woman. "Madeline loves me, and she will trust what I tell her. All we desire is a safe home. She will use the charm to help you meet your goals."

Aislin's eyes lit up for a brief moment, then

narrowed. "And how do I know she will not simply turn it against me as soon as I find her?"

"And how do you know she will not simply help Estus if he finds her first?" Alaric countered. "I've come to you in peace. If you help me, Madeline will do the same."

Aislin sighed and sunk back down to her chair, her anger suddenly gone. "So be it," she muttered. "I will help you find the girl. Just remember, your only hope for a clan lies with me, as Estus had already decided to have the girl killed."

Alaric smiled, though inside he felt sick. The Morrigan claimed that one clan still sought to use Madeline, while the other sought to kill her. He was actually surprised the one with murder on mind was Estus. Estus was an opportunist. He would never eliminate someone useful. So what were his true intentions? Alaric's stomach tightened. He preferred dealing with an enemy he *knew,* not a stranger. For the first time, he was beginning to think he never knew his enemies at all.

8

A loud banging at the door woke me. Remembering I was still in the Morrigan's Salr, I yawned, then lifted my arms to rub my groggy eyes. I didn't want to get out of bed, even with a scary goddess hammering away at my door.

I stared at the ceiling for a moment, ignoring the banging. I hadn't slept much. Every time I drifted off, I was overcome by horrible nightmares. In most of them I was fleeing from unknown, dark forms. My pursuers remained vague, but I could sense their dark intents. Had the key wielded the dreams to mess with me? Maybe, but really, the dreams felt like more of a warning than a prank. Although I could still barely sense the key, I'd probably know if it awoke to terrorize me.

Another loud set of knocks sounded on the door. I sat up, groaning at the Morrigan's impatience, as the lights slowly came on in my fully furnished room. I had no idea where the Morrigan had gotten the furniture, and I didn't want to know. I didn't want to learn anything more from her. All I wanted was to be away from the goddess as soon as possible.

As my feet hit the cold floor, I realized I wasn't alone in the room. My heart leapt into my throat, then settled back down as I realized the person crouching next to my heavy, wooden dresser was Kira. Leaning against the dresser's wooden siding, she held a finger to her lips, urging me to be quiet.

The Morrigan knocked again.

I cursed under my breath and stood, then gestured for Kira to hide under the bed. I hastily tugged the covers down to make sure she was fully concealed, then hurried to answer the door. It wasn't locked, and frankly I was surprised, yet grateful, that the Morrigan hadn't just come barging in. In fact, she even remained in the hall as I opened door.

She still wore her layers of dark clothing, with her red hair cascading nearly to her waist. However, unlike yesterday, she appeared *very* tired. Heavy bags marred the skin under her eyes, looking almost bruised against the near-translucence of her face.

"We must prepare for the ritual," she stated blandly, looking me up and down.

I instinctually wanted to take a step back, but that might invite her further into the room where she'd possibly sense Kira.

"You look tired," I commented, hoping she wouldn't take offense. "Are you sure you're up for it?"

She frowned. "This body was not made for the magic I possess. The things I've done have taken a toll."

"Maybe you should rest, er—" I paused. "You know, I really don't know what I'm supposed to call you. Is your name more of a title, or an actual name?"

She actually smiled. "You may call me Mara, and rest will not help me. I will draw strength from our army once they arrive."

I didn't like the sound of that.

She raised a red brow. "You know I can sense your emotions, my dear?"

I cringed, then shut my emotions down the way I'd learned from Mikael. I wasn't used to being around another empath, and it made me realize just how annoying I might be to everyone else.

My heart pattered nervously, but Mara didn't seem angry or offended.

"I will explain the ritual to you over breakfast," she said with a knowing smile. "Meet me when you are ready, but do not take too long."

She turned abruptly and swayed away down the hall, followed by the trail of her billowy dress and black cloak.

With a sigh of relief I shut the door, locked it, and turned back toward the room. Kira scurried out from underneath the bed, then slumped back against it in relief, still on the floor. Her green hair was alive with static from the underside of the boxspring, making her look just as frazzled as the emotions I was sensing from her. Emotions that echoed my own quite perfectly.

"What ritual?" Kira asked breathlessly. "What army?"

I moved to sit by her on the floor. "The Morrigan wants to summon an army of banshees and other phantoms to fight our enemies, other Vaettir."

I sensed a thrill of fear as it shot through her.

I turned to her. "Something tells me you know a bit about this phantom army."

Kira visibly shivered. "I remember something, from a long time ago. It seems like some distant dream."

First she remembered the Morrigan, and now this, both things that no one living should be able to recall? "Kira, just how old are you?"

She shrugged. "I remember when the lands were solid green, and the few humans respected us. I made the crops plentiful in the spring, and my sister Sivi made the rivers flow. Our patron goddess, Coventina, gave us the gifts of the wells and springs, bringing life to the land."

I inhaled so sharply that I choked on my own spit. "Sivi?" I sputtered as I tried to regain some oxygen.

Kira nodded innocently, an expression I couldn't even imagine on Sivi's face. It had to be the same Sivi, who now that I thought about it, looked quite a bit like Kira. Sivi had translucent white hair and violet eyes, but their features were nearly identical.

Sivi had been the first one to offer me a way out of Estus' Salr after I arrived. She'd later offered me a way out of his dungeon, but it would have been at the expense of many innocent lives. Sivi wanted to put things back to how they were in Kira's memories.

"She's dead," Kira clarified, interrupting my thoughts.

"Are you sure about that?" I asked weakly.

Kira nodded. "The humans took her. They had started killing our people with fire, thinking us evil. Some of us were," she added. "Things had changed by then."

Well that explained Sivi's hatred of the humans. "Did you see her die?" I asked.

Kira shook her head. "No, but if she'd survived, she would have come back for me."

"Kira," I began, gently placing my hand on her boney shoulder. I didn't want to give her false hope, but some coincidences were just too great. "I'm pretty sure I've met your sister, and she was very much alive."

She startled, then looked like she might cry. "It cannot be. She would have come for me."

I shook my head. "I'm not sure she had a choice."

Kira shivered again, clearly holding tears in. "You should go to the Morrigan," she muttered softly. "I worry she'll come back to fetch you soon."

I wanted to ask her more about the phantom army, but I'd just dropped a major bomb on her. It didn't seem right to push the subject. I sensed she wanted to be alone, so I nodded and removed my hand from her shoulder.

I stood and began to walk away, but felt compelled to turn around, overcome by a sudden wave of emotion from Kira. She remained huddled by the foot of the bed, covering her face to hide her tears, though her gentle sobs gave her away.

I wanted to go to her, but knew she wouldn't appreciate it. She'd been dealing with this pain on her own for a very long time.

I left the room, shutting the door gently behind me, then went straight to the bathroom. The small room lit up as I opened the door. Though the Salr all seemed somewhat similar, the bathroom fixtures in this one were different, more medieval. The tub was made heavy, dark metal, perhaps cast iron, and there was no toilet, just a chamber pot . . . not the most fun thing to use. On a small wooden bench by the tub were fresh clothes.

I paused to lock the door behind me, then leaned my back against it with a sigh. I'd taken a bath the previous day, and had mainly just been sitting around, so I rallied myself and went straight for the clothes. I donned the underwear and soft crimson sweater quickly. I lifted the next piece of fabric, which unfurled to reveal a long, flowy skirt, so not my style. I dropped it back to the bench, then went for the charcoal jeans I'd left in the bathroom the day before.

When I had done everything I needed in the bathroom, and could no longer stall, I left in search of the Morrigan. There had to be some way I could talk her out of the ritual. I wanted to beat Estus just as much as anyone, but I wasn't quite ready to summon a phantom army to do it.

I found Mara in the room where I'd eaten the day before. Her old book was lying open on the table, and several more had been added to it. I approached and touched one of the ancient pages while Mara remained seated by the fire.

"Where did you get these?" I asked, feeling somewhat enamored of the old books, even though they held information on a big, scary ritual.

"They were mine," she said, not turning to face me. "Preserved by my residual magic all this time. They waited for me here, hidden."

She still hadn't turned to face me, so I flipped through the pages of one of the books. The thick, waxy pages felt full of energy, making my fingertips tingle.

"Where is here, exactly?" I questioned.

I knew we were in a Salr, and that outside everything was very green, but that was the only information I had. In crow form I'd been able to perceive that we'd crossed oceans, but I wasn't sure which ones, or how far we'd actually traveled.

"This land is now called Ireland," she explained. "It is my homeland, and the land where my phantoms dwell, laid to rest within the earth."

Something about the tone of her voice was strange, almost sad, though she was shielding her emotions from me, so I couldn't be sure. There was an extra seat beside the fire, and feeling almost sympathetic, I moved away from the books and took it.

She offered me a sad smile as I sat, accepting my company. "You'll thank me for all of this in the end," she stated.

I wasn't so sure about that, but since she seemed in an information giving mood, I'd humor her.

"Why did you come back here?" I asked. At her sharp look I added, "Seriously. If this earth has changed so much from what it should have been, what value do you find in being here?"

She turned back to the fire. "You called to me."

I shook my head. "No I didn't. I didn't even know I was created in your image. Why did you come?"

She let out a long sigh, still staring into the fire. She seemed different with the fire illuminating areas of her face, almost *soft*.

"I saw an opportunity, and I took it," she answered quietly. "The old gods no longer hear the cries of their children, but I am not like them. I am no god."

Her revelation startled me. If she wasn't a goddess, how the hell had she traveled through the World Tree to get here? "If not a goddess, then what are you?"

She shrugged. "Over the centuries, many have labeled me a witch, some a goddess, and some have accused me of being one of the banshees. They are all correct, and they are all wrong."

Not fully understanding what she was saying, I waited for her to continue.

"I'm not explaining this well," she sighed, shifting in her seat. "The old gods are more like the Vaettir themselves, embodying different aspects of the earth, and of life itself, including civilization. I *am* this earth. It is a part of me. We come from the same natural balance of life, death, and emotion. It is what we are, and what you are meant to be. Harmonic balance, a never ending cycle of finding meaning, the spirit, then accepting death."

I blinked at her. " . . . *what*?"

She smiled, her gaze distant. "You will understand in time, once you have fully accepted your nature."

I shook my head, still not fully comprehending what she was, and by extension what *I* was. "But where did you *come* from? How did it happen that you were given physical form, if you *are* the earth?"

She smiled at me again. "I'm an accumulation of that energy, combined with humanity. I do not know just why I came into *physical* being, but becoming a part of humanity forced me to learn and grow as any human does. I'm the combination of humans and the earth, and all the greatnesses and terrors that such a combination can result in."

I let my breath out as I sank back into my chair.

"Do you understand?" she questioned.

I slouched down further into the cushion, feeling like I needed a hot bath, or a shot of whiskey, or *something* to take the edge off.

"Yes, and no. I mean, it makes sense to me, but if I think too hard about any of it, my brain just sort of *stops*."

Mara chuckled, then looked back toward the fire.

"I have one more question though, and I'm sorry if it sounds selfish."

She smiled and nodded.

I took her nod as a sign to go ahead and ask, "If you are the earth herself, and humanity, and emotion, then what the hell does that make me?"

She frowned for some reason, worrying me. "You are Vaettir. You are a member of your race just like any other, but you are also more. You can connect with the old, pure powers because even in this mortal form, they still flow through you. You can see things others cannot, such as the innate energy that courses through everything, and everyone, connecting us all."

I shivered despite the heat pouring forth from the fire. I *could* sense different energies, if that's what she meant, but I'd thought it was just part of being an empath. Emotion *was* energy. It was simply my gift, or my curse, nothing more.

Feeling more confused than ever, I shoved the information aside to be mulled over later. Her explanations had brought a more pertinent question to mind.

"If you are the earth and the connection within us all, why are you summoning an army to kill those we are somehow connected with?"

Her lips curved into a malicious grin, surprising me. "Because there is as much human nature in me as in any other, and vengeance and death are a part of life. We will cast our enemies down for ever thinking they are any more important than a frog, a leaf, or a tiny honey bee. I am light, but I am also darkness. We are good, but we are also evil."

I sunk even further into my chair as my heart began to race. I didn't want to be part of darkness or evil, but at that moment, I wasn't sure if I'd have a choice. All I wanted was to keep my child safe, and Alaric and Sophie. Heck, even Mikael. I was motivated by the urge to save my friends, not to crush my enemies. That was where the Morrigan and I differed.

If that made me a lesser being, then so be it. I'd never asked to be anything more than human.

Sensing my unease, Mara leaned forward, closing the space between us to put her hand over mine, which rested on the arm of my chair.

"You want to protect them, don't you?" she asked.

I inhaled deeply. I didn't know if she meant Alaric and my child, our traveling companions, or the Vaettir race in general. I was at the point where I couldn't care less about the Vaettir, but as for the others, the answer was *yes*. They had protected me, and now I needed to return the favor.

I nodded, hesitant to seal the deal with an actual *yes*.

"I can give you the power to save them all, and to save yourself," she explained, "but it has to be your choice. I was never given a choice in what came to me. I would not bestow the same fate upon you."

I quickly thought of my other options. Mikael's wife, Erykah, had said that in destroying the key, I would likely die, as would my child. One of the Norns had said the same. If I refused to put the key into my child, we would both die. Mara was the only one who'd actually given me an option where everyone would not only live, but I would be the one to save them. It would be a nice change from being such a monumental burden.

"Yes," I answered finally, placing my free hand on my belly. "I want to save them, and I will do whatever it takes."

Mara withdrew her hand and smiled. "Good. Now we must get to work. I have much to teach you before nightfall."

I let out a shaky breath and nodded. I could practically feel the gears of fate shifting. What we were going to do was against the laws of nature, and against the grim fate that had been laid before me.

So be it. I'd choose free will and survival over fate any day.

9

Crouched behind a distant tree, Sophie had watched in the darkness as her brother and James disappeared into the earth. Now, the first hints of sun were beginning to peek over the horizon. They'd been down there for hours. She glanced again through her binoculars impatiently, ignoring her weariness. She didn't like the binoculars, or anything that might hint her own senses weren't good enough, but she couldn't risk getting close enough to be seen. It could ruin everything.

If Alaric resurfaced, she would return to Mikael, setting their side of the plan into motion. If he did not, she would go in after him, despite the promises she'd made. Mikael would still be left to save Madeline, and that would have to be good enough.

She took another look through her binoculars and nearly gasped as the first figure climbed out of the earth.

Luckily, she managed to remain silent. Even at such a far distance, certain Vaettir might hear her.

She didn't recognize the first person out of the ground, a man with dark hair and copper skin, but she did recognize James as he surfaced next. She had to stifle her growl. *James.* She wished she'd had the heart to kill him, but she'd never been much of a killer unless circumstances truly called for it, despite her warlike nature. Alaric was the killer, Sophie was the tactician.

Sophie's body sagged in relief as Alaric surfaced next, followed by two other Vaettir she did not recognize. The plan must have worked. They would seek out Madeline, while Sophie and the others would prepare to aid them in any way possible, all while planning what might be the final battle for them all.

She rose and ran silently back in the direction of Mikael's current camp, wondering how her life had come to this. If only she would have stayed hidden when Alaric, Madeline, and James came looking for her in Spokane. She would have been safe . . . but no. That never would have been an option. Her brother was all she had. She'd rather follow him into hell than be alone.

She bounded across the earth tirelessly, following her own scent to find the hidden encampment. The ten miles went by quickly, though she had to stop and catch her breath right outside of the camp. Normally such a run wouldn't have fatigued her, but after the non-stop travel south, then a full night with no sleep, the long run took its toll.

Breathing easier, she ventured forth, feigning confidence to cover the aching anxiety zinging through her entire body.

Aila came into view first, her leather and fur clothing blending in well with the dried grass and oak of the forest. The only thing that stood out was her bright, blonde hair, up in its usual ponytail. Sophie observed her for a moment while Aila still couldn't see her.

The Viking warrioress hadn't spoken much since the night of the ritual. This saddened Sophie, as Aila had at some point crossed the line between traveling companion to friend. Yes, Aila had been rejected by her patron goddess, but Sophie suspected the result was based around Madeline, not Aila. Strange things had happened around Madeline since the beginning, and the attention always seemed to be on her. It wasn't surprising Madeline's goddess would come through instead of Aila's.

Finally spotting her, Aila lifted her hand in greeting. Sophie closed the distance between them as Faas and Tabitha crawled out of their tents. The few visible tents were low to the ground even when erect, their olive green coloring furthering their camouflage.

"It worked," Sophie informed Aila. "They are on the move."

"You and Mikael should go before the scent grows old," Aila advised.

Sophie nodded, not enjoying *that* aspect of the plan. She was the only one who could easily follow her brother's scent, and she would need to catch up before they reached civilization and the complications of automobiles and airplanes.

If they were able to continue following at that point, they would. If not, Mikael had given Alaric a number to call or text whenever he was able. *If* he was able. Sophie didn't like that aspect of the plan either. Aislin's people would be watching Alaric closely, and might not give him an opportunity to make contact. If that was the case, he and James would be on their own.

Mikael walked up beside Aila, wearing street clothes and a stern expression. Sophie wasn't used to seeing the expression on Mikael's face. She'd been under the impression that he'd tell jokes even if piranhas were eating him from the toes up.

"It worked?" he asked Sophie.

"James and Alaric came back out alive, with an escort," Sophie explained.

He accepted her answer with a nod. "Lead the way."

Before departing, both turned to Aila. She nodded. She would know what to do.

Sophie turned and ran back in the direction she had come, knowing Mikael would follow her.

Though she wasn't pleased with her brother being in danger, or with the ever-present threat of the key, and enemy forces, she had to admit that running through the woods felt *good*. It felt like what she was supposed to be doing. She was the embodiment of a war goddess, and also a part of nature. She was never meant to be trapped in some dark, depressing hole in the ground.

ALARIC THOUGHT he caught a glimpse of his sister watching them as they walked through the forest. He clenched his jaw against his urge to look over his shoulder again. He would have to trust Sophie would be cautious enough to remain far out of sight. If one of Aislin's people spotted her following them, the plan would be ruined, and they would all likely die.

James walked at his side, showing no signs of worry. Part of Alaric was still waiting for James to betray him, throwing him to the wolves while he went to claim Madeline himself. Of course, the plan as they'd presented it to Aislin was contingent on the fact that Alaric would convince Madeline to use the key to do Aislin's bidding. If he were dead, the plan wouldn't exactly work.

The plan wouldn't work regardless, since Madeline had about as much control over the key as anyone, but Aislin didn't need to know that. All Alaric needed was to find Madeline. If he could find her, then he'd have a chance of saving her.

When the opportunity presented itself, Mikael and Sophie would join them, and Aislin's people would likely need to be killed. *Or* the Morrigan would slaughter them all, and none of it would matter. No matter how likely such an end might be, he at least had to try.

Aislin had sent three people to accompany James and himself. He found sending such a small number odd. It was likely Aislin felt the plan might fail. She would not sacrifice any more of her people than she had to. If the plan he and James had presented was a trick, only three would die. If not, then Aislin would have Madeline and the key at her disposal. Either way, the Doyen had little to lose.

Alaric felt little guilt at the idea of killing those who accompanied them in cold blood. He knew they would do the same to him. Damon and Alejandro were the *muscle*, the former standing around six feet tall with short, honey blond hair and pale eyes, and the latter around 5'10" with perfectly copper skin, long, dark hair, and strong features hinting at his Native American heritage. Both men were well-muscled fighters. Alaric was unsure of Damon's nature, but he had learned from James that Alejandro was a descendant of Xolotl, the Aztec god of thunder.

Their third companion was Tallie, the tracker. She stood around 5'6", with straight black hair, porcelain skin, and features that spoke of the Far East. Her main talent was to track the energy signatures of others, though she could also take the form of a wolf, or so James claimed. Normally Tallie could only track someone she had interacted with, but the energy of the key was so great, she'd sensed it the moment it had been released from its former prison.

Aislin had used Tallie to track the key, and by association, Madeline, wherever she had gone, but in most cases, the search took days. The locations Tallie sensed were not exact, and she could only gain a true feel for the place if the key and Madeline remained there for several days. She had also been the one to lead Aislin to the Salr where the Norns had been slaughtered, sensing the great amount of energy used to send Alaric, Madeline, and Mikael back in time.

Aislin's troops had been on their way to the campsite where the Morrigan had been summoned, just as the Morrigan claimed, so in effect the goddess *had* saved them from a confrontation. Alaric wondered at that, since she then took Madeline away. She could have done it without the warning, leaving Alaric and the others to die.

Alaric jumped back into the present as James asked, "Are you sure you know where to find Madeline?"

Tallie glared over her shoulder at him as she continued walking. "Just because I'm not willing to share that specific information with you, does not mean I don't know where she is."

Aislin's three emissaries had all changed from their leather armor to clothes that would blend in the human world, so Alaric guessed they were either on their way to an airport or train station. Hopefully he would be able to alert Sophie once tickets were purchased, and he had an idea of where they were going.

If not, he would save Madeline on his own. He would let no one stand in his way, even the Morrigan herself.

THE OCEAN WIND hit my face, soothing my nerves, if only slightly. I watched the fading sunlight flickering on the water, hesitant to move forward. Mara stood at my side, watching me. Had I *actually* agreed to this?

We had gone over the ritual to summon the banshees countless times. Once they surfaced, other phantoms would flock to their energy, and our army would be formed.

I shivered at the thought as I looked back at the circle of rocks that marked the entrance to the Salr. The air was icy, especially with the sun slowly sinking past the horizon. It seemed odd that a place so green could also be so cold. It reminded me of Mara herself, capable of warmth and beauty, but also ruthlessness.

At some point, I'd come to believe Mara truly had what she *thought* were my best interests at heart. The banshees would protect not only me, but Alaric, Sophie, and Mikael when the time for battle came. She claimed the phantoms would be under *my* control, and would not be loosed on humanity as a whole.

While I was still nervous about the idea of being surrounded by spirits, and I hadn't quite agreed to regrowing Yggdrasil, if it could even be done, the thought of being protected by an army of my own was enough to push me into performing the needed ritual, despite my reservations. I had to do whatever would give my child the best chance at survival, if nothing else.

Before ascending to the surface, I'd found the opportunity to leave a message for Kira. I'd hidden the note in my room in hopes she would go there after we left. Once we were gone, my new friend would be able come and go from the Salr as she pleased, and my only request was that she keep an eye out for Alaric or Mikael.

She didn't understand modern technologies like telephones, and wouldn't be able to contact them even if she tried, but at least her remaining behind to keep watch gave me a small hope of them finding me.

Of course, with an army of what basically amounted to ghosts at my disposal, perhaps I would be able to find them without Mara's direct help.

I stiffened as Mara's had alighted on my shoulder. She'd seemed melancholy at best since we'd started discussing the ritual, her eyes often going distant, as if witnessing things from the far past.

She removed her hand from my shoulder then offered it to me. I took it, wrapping my fingers around hers.

A moment later we were up in the air. I mentally screamed just as much as the first time, unable to come to terms with the feeling of not having a body of my own.

Luckily, we didn't need to travel near as far this time.

Roughly ten minutes later, we swooped down toward an ancient, overgrown graveyard, separating into our human forms as our feet hit the ground. I took a deep, frantic breath, moving my hands up and down my body, then instinctually clutched my belly. It had grown dark while we travelled, but the moon was full, giving us enough light to see by.

The first thing I noticed, besides the crumbling headstones surrounding us, were the distant lights of houses. We were somewhere not far from civilization.

I looked to Mara, my worry clear on my face.

"The banshees will be under *your* command," she soothed. "They will not harm anyone unless you tell them to do so."

My shoulders slumped, but a measure of tension remained in my body. "Tell me why *I'll* be the one to command them again?"

Mara smiled patiently, her pale skin illuminated by the moonlight. "I may need to leave you for a short time. This body has weakened. I would not want to lose control of the phantoms because of my current state."

She wasn't lying. I had sensed her growing weakness like a weight pushing down on me. I knew it was almost unbearable for her, if I could sense it to such a great extent.

"You feel pity for me?" she asked, surprised.

I blushed in the darkness, still unused to keeping a constant shield up to protect my emotions.

"I can feel how tired you are," I explained.

She chuckled. "You hated me when I first took you away."

I shrugged. "I'm still mad, but I think you really do want to save me."

"And?" she pressed.

I sighed, empaths could be a real pain in the ass. "*And* maybe some of what you said about me always needing a protector somewhat made sense. It's refreshing to be around someone who thinks I'm capable of standing on my own two feet. I should never have *expected* others to help me like they have."

She grinned. "You could make the whole world bow at your feet, if you so chose."

I laughed. "Let's not get carried away. I want to save my loved ones, and sever my connection with the key. That's it."

She nodded. "Then that is what you will do, all on your own."

I nodded in return, then took a deep breath. "Are we ready?"

She let out a breath of her own, and if I didn't know any better, I would have said she was nervous.

She reached both of her hands out to me. I grasped them in my own, forming a circle with our arms. A cool breeze played with my loose hair. It tickled my face, distracting me, though my distraction only lasted for a moment as Mara closed her eyes and began to chant.

I joined in, repeating the words I'd memorized, first invoking the cardinal directions. The chant reminded me of something from modern day witch movies, except it was in Gaelic, the Morrigan's chosen tongue. The pronunciation had come more natural to me than Old Norsk, but it still had been difficult to get down. Fortunately it was a short chant, and having Mara say it with me helped.

I felt power growing around us, but words were only half the battle. Mara had explained that rituals weren't just about the words, they were about *intent*. You could mutter magic words all night long, but if you didn't have both the intent and power to back them up, all you would end up with was a lost voice from too much chanting.

We continued the chant, then started it anew from the beginning.

We finished, and repeated it a third time. That we were repeating it yet again was probably my fault. I wasn't focused. I still had reservations about what we were doing, and my mind was too consumed with thoughts of Alaric, and what might be going on with the budding war while I was with Mara.

She stopped chanting and eyed me in the darkness. "This body is too weak to complete the ritual on its own. I need your help."

I frowned. "I'm trying. I just can't seem to focus."

Mara sighed. "I can feel that you're trying, I apologize. Sometimes I forget you do not have the same experiences as I. Complete focus is a skill many mortals never attain. I can't expect you to have honed such a skill in your short lifetime."

I pulled away and dropped my hands to my sides. "So what do we do?"

Mara laughed, though it was weak. I could feel bone-aching tiredness wafting off her, making me feel tired too, though I was well rested.

"It weakens me being on this earth without my true form," she explained at my worried expression. "That form was lost to me long ago. I know it is wrong for me to be here, but I *needed* to help you. I needed to right the unbalance I helped create."

"But—" I began, wondering at her words.

She held up a hand to stop me. "We must try again."

I held my hands out to her reluctantly. If she didn't have the strength to perform such a ritual, there was no way I'd be able to do it.

Her eyes bored into mine as our arms formed a circle once more. "Close your eyes," she instructed.

I did as she bade me, feeling nervous. I'd always felt uncomfortable keeping my eyes closed when I wasn't going to sleep. Like something was going to jump out and attack me if I didn't keep an ever vigilant watch.

"Breathe deeply," she continued as I forced my eyes to remain shut. "Taste the moisture in the air. Feel the plants around us."

I took a deep breath, and felt a measure of calm. When I really focused, I *could* sense the plants around us, and the tiny little lives of animals and bugs. It was all energy, just like the force that flowed through humans and Vaettir alike.

"Good," Mara commented. "Continue to feel the energy. Search outward, and search downward. Focus on all that we're surrounded by."

I did as she bade, and eventually complete calm washed over my body.

"Now chant," she said softly.

I chanted, no longer worried about forgetting the foreign words. They came naturally to my tongue, as if I'd been speaking them all my life. I felt pressure building as we named each direction once again, asking for the earth and sky to grant us their energy. I'd never been overly pagan in my spirituality, but the answering energies left little doubt there was something to the idea of earth magic. The energies were too tangible, too *real*, to be ignored.

The key remained quiet all the while, to my great relief. It hadn't chimed in for ages, as if afraid . . . or else it was just waiting for the right moment. Perhaps I was doing just as it wanted.

The thought gave me pause, momentarily severing my connection from nature, but it was too late. A final burst of energy erupted between our bodies, blowing our hair away from our faces in perfect unison.

The energy grew between us, but nothing else was happening. No phantoms came into existence.

Mara suddenly pulled away from me. I reached out

for her, surprised. She hadn't said anything about pulling away during the ritual.

A gleaming knife appeared in her hand, held steady as the loose fabric of her clothing whipped around her like a mini hurricane. I reared away from her, fearful I'd been betrayed, then she plunged the blade through her ribcage, directly into her heart. I felt it as the blade connected with the vital organ, like I had been stabbed myself.

I coughed, thinking that it was only my empathy affecting me, but my hand came away with blood. I fell to my knees, mirroring Mara. Blood trickled from her lips as her eyes met mine.

"The ritual connects us, and it calls for death," she croaked. "Take my energy," she instructed. "Finish this."

We simultaneously coughed up more blood and I reached out for her. My hands connected with her bloody chest. I could feel her frantic life force reaching out to me. It had nothing to do with whatever life had previously been in the corpse. It was all Mara, the same energy that had travelled through the spectral tree and into Sophie. I didn't understand how I could release that much life force, a life force capable of surviving on its own, and jumping from host to host.

Our faces were only inches away from each other. "I have grown too weak to maintain myself. Give me form when it is time," she whispered. "You are much stronger than I ever was."

Her life force rushed into me. The pain left me, and I

knew just what I was supposed to do. I sent a wave of energy into the ground, just like I had done when I raised the corpses that initially protected the key. Something answered, a distant echo in my head, as Mara's body slumped to the earth beside me.

Misty shapes emerged from the soil, surrounding me so that I could barely see past them. They wore cloaks that seemed to be made of swirling smoke. Inside the cloaks, spectral features slowly formed. They were all women, with long, incorporeal hair swirling in the breeze to meld with their cloaks.

"Why have you awoken us?" several voices asked in my head. It felt like when I "spoke" to any other dead. There really were no words, but the point was conveyed regardless.

I opened my mouth to instruct the banshees, but was cut off as the key came to life inside me. I was held immobile as something that wasn't me said, "To spill the blood of my enemies."

"As you wish, Morrigan," the banshees echoed in my head.

I didn't know if the banshees were talking to me, the key, or the Morrigan's energy still within me, but I didn't have time to think about it. The three energies fought against each other, making me feel like they might burst through my skin any moment. I couldn't contain such immense power in my mortal form. There was no way.

As the energies collided with each other in one final shove, I screamed, clawing at my face in agony.

Still on my knees, I fell the rest of the way to the ground. The damp soil was moist and soothing, even though distantly I knew that my cheek was resting against a gravestone.

Beyond the immense energy within me, I could feel the energy of the earth below me. I reached out, focusing on that calm force instead of the war inside me. It soothed the three of us, as it called out to each form of energy equally. We were all different, yet we were all a part of the earth. We could work together. We were *supposed* to work together.

Suddenly all felt still. The earth, life, death, emotion, and chaos had suddenly found balance, just as they had found a purpose.

10

J ames and Alaric had been led to the Oslo Airport, where they now waited to board their flight. It was the same airport that had first welcomed them to Norway, and it brought back nostalgic memories for Alaric.

On that original flight, Madeline had slept on his shoulder almost the entire way, giving him hope she would forgive him. It had been one of the happiest moments he'd had in many years, and he'd always remember it fondly, especially because it was one of the last days before Madeline came in contact with the key. He wished he could rewind to that flight right in that moment. He doubted his upcoming flight would be anywhere near as enjoyable.

"What are you doing?" Alejandro demanded, walking up beside Alaric.

Alaric startled. He hadn't heard Alejandro's approach

in the noisy airport boarding area. He raked his fingers through his hair and offered Alejandro a lazy smile, pretending he had just been daydreaming, when really he'd been trying to drop a note in a trash can for Sophie. He knew she would be somewhere near the airport, and would be able to smell out anything he left for her. She would not be pleased about digging through a trash can, but it seemed his best option if he didn't want Damon, Alejandro, or Tallie to notice the note before they departed.

He glanced over at James, relaxing in the first of several rows of waiting room seats. His muscled arms were spread out onto the seats on either side of him, taking up way more space than was necessary. He was so still he could have almost been asleep. It was hard to tell for sure with the dark sunglasses shielding his eyes. Either way, he wasn't likely to be much help.

"Just wondering why I'm not allowed to hold my own ticket," Alaric replied, letting his irritation show in his voice.

Really, he had no need to hold the ticket. Even though he'd had to wait near the airport's entrance while Tallie purchased plane tickets for all, with his heightened hearing he'd heard her booking their flight to Dublin, Ireland. That was what he'd written on the crumpled napkin that was now back within his pocket.

"You'll find out where we're going soon enough," Damon grumbled as he came to stand on Alaric's other side, nervously pushing his honey blond hair back from his face. "For now, we'd rather like to delay the moment where you try to kill us."

Alaric dramatically lifted a hand to his chest. "Do you truly think so little of me?"

Before Damon could reply, Alejandro smirked. "We are *all* on Aislin's bad side. This is our last chance to come through for her. If it's a trap, you'll just be saving Aislin the trouble of killing us herself."

"Shut up," Tallie ordered as she joined them, a large, soft pretzel in hand.

"What does it matter?" Alejandro sighed, glancing over at Tallie. "I'm sure he already figured out where we're going. We can fight to the death now, or later. What's the difference?"

Though Alejandro was correct, Alaric didn't quite feel the need to rub it in. Instead he kept quiet, hoping to keep the trio in an argumentative state where they might give away more information. His hopes were dashed as James chuckled from where he sat behind them, bringing everyone's attention to him.

"What is so damned funny?" Tallie asked hotly, turning away from Alejandro to aim her dark eyes at James.

James smirked, remaining in a relaxed, seated position. "You're all *so* worried that Aislin has purposefully put you into a position to be killed. Imagine what she'll do to *me* if I somehow end up fooling all of you. A quick death would be a reward compared to what might be in store for me. You all should be grateful."

"Is that an admission of guilt?" Tallie growled, turning away from the rest of the group to stalk toward James.

James grinned, though it was more a bearing of teeth, predator to predator. "Not quite."

Annoyed with the entire situation, Alaric looked up at the flight board. They were congregated in the wrong section of the airport, a weak attempt by Tallie to keep him and James in the dark. He knew which plane they needed to board, and when. Their flight was the next in line, and he hadn't managed to leave any clues for Sophie. With how Alejandro was watching him, he doubted he'd be given any opportunities.

"Why even try?" Alaric muttered, more voicing his own frustration than anything.

Tallie turned away from James to eye him dangerously. "If we succeed, we will be back in Aislin's good graces. If we fail, we will die. If we don't try at all, or if we run, we will end up with fates far worse than death. I have no doubt Aislin would find us, no matter where we hid, or with whom."

Damon and Alejandro silently nodded in agreement. Alaric was beginning to think Estus wasn't the only Doyen who didn't really care about the best interests of other Vaettir. He flashed back on the nervous blonde guard in Aislin's Salr, followed by the wary glances of her people as they walked through the halls. A tyrant is a tyrant is a tyrant. They might have come in different packages, but Estus and Aislin were very much the same.

126

A little beep sounded as the airport's intercom came to life. A voice announced it was time to board the flight to Dublin.

Alaric feigned surprise as Damon shoved him ahead of the rest of the group. They crossed the center hall to the correct waiting area. Damon smiled smugly as they filed into line with the other passengers. Alejandro moved up to Alaric's other side, giving him a look that said, *drop the act*. Alaric smiled knowingly at Alejandro and nodded.

Turning his gaze forward, Alaric fingered the napkin in his pocket. Since they were surrounded by distracting humans, he briefly considered dropping it on the ground, but it was too risky. If one of the others found it, they'd know the trap was coming that they already half-expected. He needed a more finite location on Madeline before that confrontation took place.

Gritting his teeth in annoyance, he boarded the plane.

I HAD no idea how much time had passed since the earth's soothing energy overcame me. When I finally sat up, it was still dark, and the banshees still watched me with hollow eyes.

Mara's dead body was beside me, and I knew I better high tail it out of the cemetery before any humans decided to visit their loved ones. As I looked down at her corpse, her words echoed in my head, *Give me form when it's time.*

I had no idea what she meant. The body she'd "killed" had already died once. It wasn't her real body, so maybe she'd just find a new one . . . but then, why had she asked *me* to give her form? Had her essence weakened too much for her to simply find another body, or was her last body's death some sort of sacrifice? Did she give up more in the ritual than just her borrowed form?

The questions were making my head spin, especially since I'd likely never get a definite answer. I rose to my feet as the banshees watched me curiously. Now that I was able to fully focus on them, I could tell their faces were actually very different, though they were all female. They floated above the earth in diaphanous robes, but I could still tell that some were taller than others, and some had larger or smaller frames. These were real women once, and now they were tortured souls. I could feel them just like I could feel the remaining energy in one of the Vaettir after their body had died. The banshees were trapped, anchored to the earth. It kept them from moving on.

I felt a connection to them, just like I did with other dead. I knew I could command them. I could sense their desire for a purpose. Thoughts suddenly flashed through my mind, and I wasn't sure if they came from the key, or from whatever part of the Morrigan was now inside me. It was confusing trying to decipher the difference, so instead I just listened to what the thoughts were trying to convey.

Our army must grow, they said.

I frowned. It was a thought both the Morrigan and the key would have, but I only wanted to listen if it was Mara telling me to do it. Anything the key wanted would be evil . . . yet it seemed to be going along with our plan. It had shown me it still had the ability to take over, to make me speak words that were not my own, yet it had kept quiet as we planned to summon Freyja, perhaps knowing we would get the Morrigan instead. Then it had kept quiet as Mara and I planned the ritual to summon the banshees. I was obviously playing right into what the key wanted, and I wasn't sure if that was a good thing or a bad thing.

"I don't know what comes next," I said out loud.

Realistically I needed to get out of that graveyard, and I needed to grow an army, but I didn't know *how* to do either of those things.

We know the way, one of the banshees chimed in, her voice an eerie whisper in my mind.

We can take you, another explained, her voice far deeper than the first.

"I need to find Alaric," I replied out loud.

No, not yet, a voice echoed in my head. It wasn't one of the banshees, rather a voice from within me. It made me dizzy to listen to so many forms of input directly into my brain. I clutched at my stomach, feeling nauseous.

"I need to do this on my own," I muttered, surprised, because I was pretty sure that it was *my* thought.

This fight had become extremely personal, especially with two foreign entities in my head, and one growing in my belly. It was the latter that made me realize I needed to step up to the plate.

My daughter would have Alaric, Sophie, and perhaps even others to protect her eventually, but right now, what she had was *me*. I needed to be strong enough to not only protect her, but to eventually show her that she could protect herself.

The banshees edged closer to me. I noticed a light swooping back and forth in the distance, and I realized with a start that someone was walking toward the graveyard with a flashlight. Someone had probably heard me talking to myself, and wanted to make sure no one was out here defacing the graves.

The banshees were suddenly very close. *We must go,* one of them urged. The image of a woman turning into a crow swept through my mind, but I shook my head. I wasn't the Morrigan. *That* gift was beyond me.

They seemed to sigh, then suddenly I was enveloped in mist. I had the sensation of flying, though I couldn't see nor feel much else. It wasn't as frightening as when I'd traveled with Mara. My body still felt whole as I was lifted into the air, just somewhat incorporeal.

The next thing I knew, I was standing in another dark graveyard. This one was deep within a forest. Most of the gravestones were nothing but chunks of stone on the ground, but I could feel the graves underneath. They weren't like regular graves. They were . . . restless.

They are not like us, one of the banshees explained, *but they will come if you call. They will fight.*

I felt confused again as reality seeped in. It was like I was alternating between a trance state, and the real me. The banshees' energy was overwhelming, as were the energies inside me. The spirits in the ground called out to the part of me that was *death*, but that was not all that I was. I was also life, and I couldn't forget that.

We only recognize death, one of the banshees whispered through my mind. *It holds us in its eternal embrace. It is all that we are.*

I sensed the truth in her words. The banshees would bring death and darkness, because it was all they knew. They followed me because they recognized one of their own, at least in part.

Call to them, the banshees instructed as one.

I did as they bade me. It hardly took any effort, since the spirits were already reaching out to me, begging to be released. I had a moment of worry over what might happen if I lost control of the dead I was collecting, but the thought washed away as the spirits joined us. Most were barely visible, but the change in energy was dramatic. It radiated through me, making me want *more*.

I could feel the key's excitement. It was no longer bothering to shield itself from me. We had a dual purpose now, even if we were acting for different reasons. It was sure it could take over if I faltered, though

I didn't entirely agree. I was frightened by the idea, but I thought that maybe, just maybe, I'd be strong enough to fight it. The dead were mine, after all. They did not answer to the chaos that was the key.

Without another word, the banshees closed around me. After several dizzying moments, we reached the next set of ancient graves. These had no headstones at all. They'd never had them. It was a mass grave. The spirits were all tangled together underneath the earth.

I called to them, and they answered, pleased to be released from below.

We continued on, from graveyard to graveyard. I began to get a sense that *all* of these spirits recognized the Morrigan. She had used them before, and they had waited for centuries, anxious for the moment she would come again. Phantom Queen indeed.

They weren't normal spirits, either. Normal spirits found their peace and moved on. These wanted *more*. They could not let go of the lives they had once lived, just like the banshees.

We moved on to the next graveyard, traveling a much greater distance, then on to the next, growing my army every time my feet hit the ground. Eventually other creatures began to join us. Creatures that shouldn't exist in the modern day world flocked to the gathering energy, awoken from what should have been an eternal slumber.

I couldn't make them out clearly in the night. Most often, I would just catch a glimpse of bat-like wings in my peripheral vision, or perhaps a glowing set of eyes here and there.

As our communal power grew, I began to feel like we might actually succeed. We might win against Estus, and Aislin. My child and I might survive.

As I stood in another graveyard, looking around at the army I had amassed in record time, I felt almost smug. There was a new Phantom Queen in town.

11

A fter arriving in Dublin well after midnight, Alaric, James, and Aislin's trio traveled by car to the North. *Far* North. Tallie drove, still unwilling to give away Madeline's location.

She seemed overly anxious during the car ride, giving Alaric the impression that more was wrong than previously stated. He hoped the *wrongness* had nothing to do with what Tallie could sense of the key and Madeline. At the very least, it could be that Madeline had already left wherever she had been, leaving Tallie to trace only the residual energy of her prolonged stay. At the very worst . . . well, he didn't like to think about the worst. He *couldn't* think about the worst.

After several hours, they arrived in a remote area near the coast, just as the first rays of morning sun appeared. Their plane had landed in the middle of the night, but none of them had voiced concern over rest as they immediately picked up their rental car and began driving. Luckily Ireland was a small country.

They emerged from the car to stand amongst a countryside awash with green. The ocean surf sounded in the distance. Alaric and the other men followed Tallie's lead like silent shadows.

She walked on for ten minutes, utterly absorbed in her task, but eventually stopped to look around, confused. Sensing Tallie's unease, Alaric surveyed the countryside anxiously. Had she lost the trail?

He scented the air. Madeline's scent was everywhere, but faint. She hadn't been there in several hours, if not more. He turned his gaze back to Tallie, searching amongst large chunks of rock for an exact location.

The search went on for another twenty minutes. Unable to stand idly by any longer, Alaric approached Tallie's side, leaving the other men to wait in silence behind him. She continued looking down at the ground. Alaric wasn't sure if she was actually looking for something, or just trying to bar any conversation.

"She's not here anymore, is she?" he asked softly, leaning forward into Tallie's gaze so she couldn't ignore him.

She tilted her chin down enough that her long, black hair covered her delicate features, then continued walking forward.

"Answer me," he demanded, catching up to her side once more.

She turned her panicked face up to him. "No," she

breathed, "but we can at least look for clues to indicate where she went. She hasn't remained in one place long enough for me to locate her again."

Alaric let out the breath he'd been holding. At least she was still alive. He could deal with her not being where they'd hoped, as long as she still lived.

He looked over his shoulder, sensing eyes on him, but the others remained back where he'd left them, looking bored. He glanced around the greenery and stones, sure there was someone else around, but his eyes found nothing.

"What is it?" Tallie asked suspiciously.

"Someone is here," he whispered.

The rustle of a nearby patch of brambles piqued his senses. He turned his gaze in search of the source, knowing he would feel extremely silly if it turned out to be an animal. Still, he couldn't shake the feeling that he'd had eyes on him.

Movement caught his attention once more. "There," he whispered, pointing to a copse of small, scraggly trees.

Before he could react, Tallie leapt through the air, shifting fluidly into a wolf before she hit the ground. Alaric had seen other Vaettir shift before, and was capable of small changes himself, but a shift like that . . . he'd only seen once.

His jaw clenched at the thought of the Morrigan turning effortlessly into a crow. He didn't know how she'd transported Madeline along with her in that form, but he was sure she did, given there was no scent trail to follow on the frozen ground back where Madeline had first disappeared.

He shook away his morose feelings as the giant wolf that was formerly Tallie darted around large stones, making a beeline for the copse of trees. Cursing his hesitation, he darted after her, hoping she wouldn't kill whatever she found. Distantly he heard the rest of their group jogging to catch up behind them.

He reached the copse of trees a moment later to find Tallie, still in wolf form, pinning something to the ground. No, not something, *someone*. The woman was tiny, with long green hair and angular features. She wore bulky, mismatched clothes, and seemed almost childlike. Judging by her scent, she was Vaettir.

Ignoring the snarling wolf on top of her, she turned wide eyes up to Alaric. "*You*," she whispered. "Are you really him?"

He took a step closer as the others reached them. "Am I really who?" he asked suspiciously.

"Maddy's boyfriend," the tiny woman answered, her voice strained from the crushing presence of the wolf.

Alaric's heart fell to his toes, then shot back up again in elation. "Get off her!" he demanded, shoving Tallie aside.

Tallie immediately returned to human form, her clothes reappearing as if by magic, just like the Morrigan's had. Her rump in the grass, she glared up at him.

Ignoring her, Alaric reached down to offer the small,

frightened woman a hand up. She looked hesitantly at his outstretched hand, then took it. Once up on her feet, she took back her hand and stepped away from him.

"What do you know about Madeline?" he demanded, his heart still fighting to beat out of his chest. "Where did she go?"

The woman bit her lip. "So you're really him then? Alaric? Where is Mikael?"

Alaric frowned at the mention of Mikael, but quickly brushed the uncomfortable feeling aside. "Mikael is not here. Now *please* tell me where Madeline is. Time may be running out."

The woman nodded. Everyone stood silent as she explained, "The Morrigan took her away yesterday evening. I don't know where they were going, but Maddy left me a note. She said if I saw you or Mikael, I should tell you she's alright, that the Morrigan won't hurt her, but that she hopes to find you soon. She didn't know where they were going."

"One day," Alaric breathed. "We missed them by *one* day," he said more loudly, overwhelmingly frustrated.

"Will they return to this place?" Alejandro cut in as he took a step toward the small woman.

Alaric was glad for the interruption, and the logical question. He felt like he was about to lose his mind, or maybe he already had.

The little woman shook her head in response to Alejandro. "I don't know. The Morrigan left her books behind, maybe she'll come back for them."

"Books?" Alaric questioned, grasping at any small details that might tell him where Madeline had gone.

The woman's face lit up as she nodded, excited to be of use.

It was clear to Alaric that Madeline had befriended the strange woman, and he was not at all surprised. Madeline seemed to make friends under the most unusual of circumstances.

"Follow me," she said happily, then hurried right past Tallie, apparently unafraid that Tallie could shift back into a wolf and eat her.

Alaric was the first to run after her, followed a moment later by the others.

"My name is Kira," the woman explained as they jogged along over the loamy earth.

Her short legs belied the fact that she was incredibly fast. Alaric had to run at full speed to keep up with her as she darted around rocks, her long, green hair streaming behind her.

Kira suddenly came to such an abrupt stop that he ran right past her. He skidded to a halt, then turned to see her standing amongst a circle of large rocks. "And this is my home," she explained breathily.

Alaric took a step toward her, wondering what she was talking about. He had his answer a moment later as Kira bent down to touch something on the ground. Alaric tensed as he began to sink into the earth, then relaxed when he realized Kira was sinking too. Within a minute they were below the earth, standing in the entrance of a Salr.

"Are there other Vaettir here?" he asked cautiously.

He glanced around the dimly lit room. They'd entered the earth ahead of the others, leaving Alaric suddenly alone with Kira, vulnerable to an ambush.

She shook her head. "It was just me for a very long time, then Maddy and the Morrigan came. Maddy helped to keep me hidden. She didn't know what the Morrigan would do if she found me."

"Where can I find the books you mentioned?" he interrupted, anxious to look for clues now that he knew there was no danger, unless Kira was lying, but he didn't think she was.

Kira nodded, then started forward out of the small entry room, leading the way down a long hall. There was a commotion behind him as the others figured out how to enter the Salr, but he didn't bother waiting for them.

Kira led him to a large, cozy room with a heavy, wood table, comfy furniture, and a massive fireplace. He could still smell the smoke and ash of a recent fire. Books lined the large table, recently placed, judging by the dust that had been swept from them. He still couldn't believe he'd just barely missed Madeline, though the proof was all around.

The books now in his sights, Alaric rushed forward and began leafing though the pages while Kira stood aside. He could smell Madeline all over the ancient parchment, and the Morrigan too. They had studied these books together.

He frowned as the contents of the pages became clear. They were books of necromancy, or something like it, filled with rituals to summon the dead. He couldn't decipher them fully, as the text was in Gaelic, but he'd spent ample time in his five hundred years learning languages, and knew enough Gaelic to get the gist.

With a sigh, he stepped away from the books, hoping Madeline hadn't let the Morrigan talk her into something foolish. "Where is the note she left you?" he asked numbly, his back still to Kira.

"In her room," she answered, drawing Alaric's attention to her face. She suddenly seemed sad.

"Show me," he demanded.

She nodded, then ran off again with Alaric hot on her heels. A moment later they arrived in a bedroom. Madeline's scent was everywhere, and the bedding was still mussed from the last time she'd slept there. It was all almost too much. If they'd gone to Aislin just a little bit sooner . . .

Suddenly Kira was at his side, poking his arm to get his attention. She handed him a crumpled note.

He took it gingerly and flattened it in his hands. It read:

KIRA,

I'm sorry I had to leave you here alone, but I'm guessing

it's how you like things to be. You should be able to leave the Salr now to visit your human friends. I would like to let you just get back to normal life, but I have to ask you a favor.

My boyfriend, Alaric, is searching for me. I don't know if he will make it this far, but I can't miss the chance if he does. If he comes, you will recognize him by his long, black hair and dark eyes. He's very handsome, and is also Vaettir, like us. He might be with a woman who looks very similar to him, and another man, this one very tall, with long, reddish hair and eyes almost just as red. His name is Mikael. If you see either of them, please tell them that I'm okay. The Morrigan is trying to help me, and I think she knows what she's doing. I'm trusting in that idea, as I have no other choice. Once I am able, I will come looking for them. Alaric will have trouble finding me since we're traveling by . . . unusual means. If he still chooses to try, all I can tell him is that I believe we will remain on this continent for a while.

Tell him I love him, and that our daughter is doing just fine. At his stunned expression, clarify to him that yes, I said daughter. I think we might have a way to win this war, and to control the key, but I cannot say any more for fear this letter will fall into the wrong hands.

Once this is all over, if I am able, I will return here, and bring you to your sister if you so choose. Just be aware, she may not be the sister you once knew.

Y*OUR* F*RIEND ALWAYS,*

> *Madeline*

P.S. If you see any other Vaettir besides Alaric or Mikael, please do not approach them as you did me. They may mean you harm.

ALARIC LET out his breath as he reread the hastily scrawled words. They were a small consolation, but at least he knew Madeline and their child had been well when she wrote the letter. He shook his head. Not just their child. Their *daughter*. He felt an overwhelming mixture of elation, paired with crushing fear. He *would* save them.

Alaric reread the letter again, barely aware of James and Alejandro as they entered the room behind him.

"Did you see the books?" James questioned.

Alaric turned and nodded, almost wishing he had taken the time to hide the books from the others. He didn't want to give Aislin any clues as to what might happen in the near future.

"We need to find her quickly," he stated.

Both James and Alejandro nodded in reply. Alejandro looked worried. James just looked like James. Cold and dispassionate.

Tallie and Damon appeared in the doorway behind them.

"Let's go," Tallie ordered.

Alaric didn't like taking orders, but this one he had

no problem obeying. He needed to find Madeline, to stop her from doing whatever she might be doing, before it was too late.

SOPHIE SAT next to Mikael on the plane, breathing in the stale airplane air, tinged with a smell like antiseptic. She hated flying at the best of times, and her traveling companion wasn't making it any easier. He had requested numerous plastic cups of wine from the steward over the course of the flight, and was beginning to seem a little drunk.

"Is now really the time for that?" Sophie questioned, as he ordered what must have been his tenth glass. She'd lost count at some point, and had a suspicion he'd snuck more in while she'd been deep in thought.

He frowned at her, then sighed as he leaned back against his seat, reclining it the small amount allowed.

"Flying makes me nervous," he admitted.

Sophie's eyes widened.

"What?" he asked, sounding almost embarrassed, though Sophie felt he was incapable of *true* embarrassment.

She shook her head, then grabbed her seltzer water to take a sip. Flying made her queasy, just like riding in the backseat of a car, though she'd never outwardly admit weakness in either situation. "Nothing," she answered, returning her seltzer to the little tray attached to the seat in front of her, "just surprised you actually admitted that to me."

He grinned, transitioning easily back into the Mikael she was used to. "Come now, we're practically family."

Sophie glared, thinking she liked the embarrassed Mikael better. "*No* we are not. Alaric is my only family."

"And Madeline?" he pressed, leaning toward her, a small, knowing smile on his face. "She's carrying your niece or nephew. Is she not family?"

Sophie ground her teeth in annoyance. "Yes," she answered grudgingly. "Madeline is family."

It was the truth. When Sophie had found the note in the trash can, covered in James' scent, she had been elated by the idea that she'd be able to help rescue Madeline and her unborn child, especially since she'd almost given up hope.

She'd purchased a plane ticket just so she could follow Alaric's scent to the boarding area. But as she scoured everything he'd touched, she found no clue as to where he had gone. It was only when she switched gears and started scenting James that she found the note. It had been more than surprising. Perhaps leaving James alive hadn't been the *worst* idea after all.

"We better be able to find them," she muttered to herself, her thoughts turning back to Alaric and Madeline.

Thinking she was talking to him, Mikael replied, "I have many contacts in Ireland. Hopefully someone will have seen *something*. Unless you think you can sniff your brother out."

Sophie huffed. "Only if they're traveling on foot. If they rented a car at the airport, I have no way of locating him."

Mikael nodded. "My connections it is. Many reside in Dublin, so that will be our first stop."

Sophie frowned and leaned back against her seat. "They better be damn good connections."

Mikael looked smug as he received his umpteenth plastic cup of wine. "Everything I do is damn good," he replied. "You should know that by now."

Mikael *had* gotten them farther than Sophie had thought possible, so she supposed she could give credit where credit was due . . . though she'd never give it out loud.

12

Alaric inhaled the coastal breeze as they exited the Salr. The sky outside had grown cloudy, changing the pressure and making everything feel crisp with moisture. He gazed out toward the coastline as the others joined him.

Tallie wrapped her arms around herself, making the black leather of her coat groan. She gazed up at the clouds warily.

"That sure was an abrupt weather change," Damon commented.

Alaric ignored him, though he was thinking the same thing. He began walking back toward the car, expecting the others to follow. They'd searched the rest of the Salr to little avail, gaining nothing of use in their quest for Madeline. He was anxious to start searching elsewhere.

According to Tallie, Madeline had been on the move all night, and great amounts of energy were gathering wherever she went. Tallie felt the energy clusters were enough that she could probably lead them to one of the places, but it might be a worthless venture, as Madeline had not stayed put in any place for long, likely leaving few clues, if any.

They were going to the nearest site regardless, as it was better than just waiting at the mostly-abandoned Salr. If Tallie sensed Madeline again, they would simply change course.

They were halfway to the car when the air pressure changed dramatically, making Alaric's ears pop. The temperature immediately dropped by ten degrees, and the sky darkened further.

"Do you feel that?" Tallie hissed, halting in her tracks.

Alejandro looked up at the sky, his long hair whipping away from his face as the wind picked up. "It feels like standing too close to lightning. Like there are electric currents running from the sky to the earth around us."

Alaric shifted from foot to foot uneasily as the hairs raised on his bare arms. His attention was drawn back to the coast. Something was moving out there, like a large, swirling mass of low, dark clouds.

After staring at the coastline for several minutes, he walked toward the dark scene. A horrible feeling compressed his lungs as his entire body erupted with goosebumps.

"Where are you going?" Tallie asked breathlessly. "Whatever this is, we don't want to confront it."

Ignoring her, Alaric increased his pace to a jog, trusting his intuition. Whatever the swirling mass was, it had something to do with Madeline. Once he had closed some of the distance, *she* came into view. He knew it was her, even without being close enough to see her features.

Dark shapes swirled around, darting in and out of the mass that seemed to move with Madeline's slender form. At first it had seemed like she was floating with them, almost melding with their diaphanous shapes, then she touched down onto the sandy shore and began to walk.

Alaric raced toward her, heedless of the phantoms.

"Madeline!" he called, loud enough to be heard over the crashing ocean waves as he neared the beach where Madeline stood.

Her eyes rose to his as he halted his progress, about twenty feet away from her. She wore a crimson sweater and gray jeans that looked out of place with her supernatural entourage.

Panic clawed at his throat as Madeline stared at him. He feared she'd been taken over by the key, or worse, the Morrigan. Then she smiled.

"I knew you'd find me!" she called out.

He darted forward, closing the rest of the distance between them. His feet sunk into the soft sand as he wrapped her up in his arms. The phantoms swirled around them both as he kissed her, unable to help himself, though he had a million questions.

When he finally pulled away, he whispered, "What have you done?"

She smiled again. "I've built an army to protect us and our child."

"How?" he asked, glancing up at the dark forms. "*Why?*"

The unnatural wind played with his hair, melding it with Madeline's as he held her close. She didn't feel entirely real in his arms. Everything felt like a dream, at least, he hoped it was a dream, and not a nightmare.

He wasn't one to scare easily, but he had to admit, the phantoms had him on edge, even *if* they were under Madeline's control like they seemed to be. He didn't know how to fight phantoms, or if he even could. He was a warrior at heart, and intangible entities unnerved him.

She frowned. "What do you mean, *why*? I couldn't rely on you to protect me forever. I know you all think I'm weak, but I'm not."

"I know you're not weak," he gasped, confused by the accusation in her words, "but this?" he added removing an arm from around her waist to gesture at the sky.

She watched him with a hurt expression, not bothering to glance up at the phantoms. Maybe she wasn't entirely herself after all.

Seeing that his current tactics were getting him nowhere, he changed his approach, though it pained him to do so.

"Where is the Morrigan?" he questioned evenly.

Her expression crumbled. "She sacrificed her human form to summon the banshees. I will bring her back when the time comes."

Her words didn't make sense. Something was *very* wrong, but Alaric felt it prudent not to comment. It would probably be a good thing if the Morrigan was truly gone, and stayed gone.

Not voicing his opinion was difficult, but he didn't want Madeline getting mad and taking off with her phantoms. The *real* Madeline wouldn't run, but he had no idea who he was actually dealing with in that moment.

He returned his arm to her waist to hold her a little tighter, just in case, then calmly asked, "What do you plan next?"

Relaxing into his embrace, she explained, "We must plan the final battle. From that I will gather enough energy to separate myself from both the Morrigan and the key."

The relief he'd felt when Madeline relaxed in his arms was instantly wiped away at her words. Had the Morrigan somehow shielded herself within Madeline, just like the key? That had to be the case if Madeline needed to *separate* herself from her.

"Where is Mikael?" she asked.

He clenched his jaw, wanting to say *something*, or to at least lash out at the Morrigan in some way, but instead he answered Madeline's question.

"I wasn't able to send word to him before coming here. He is likely still back in Norway, waiting for a phone call."

She didn't seem to hear his words as she turned her gaze past him. Alaric glanced back to see Aislin's people, waiting on the crest of a hill, but James had left them and was heading their way.

"Who are they?" Madeline whispered, referring to those remaining on the hill.

"They belong to Aislin," he explained, turning his attention back to Madeline in his arms. "Joining with them was the only way I could find you."

She nodded, seeming to accept his answer, then pulled away as James approached. Alaric turned to stand beside her, facing James.

"He has his memories back," Madeline observed once James was within hearing range, surprising Alaric with her insight.

"I sure do," James said as he reached them, stopping before he reached the phantoms. "And I know who killed my grandmother."

Alaric turned his head to watch Madeline's expression. If she was nervous, it didn't show. The old Madeline would have been nervous.

"You'll get over it."

One of the phantoms darted toward James. He stumbled back, cowering as more of the dark forms swooped toward him, *threatening*.

"I suppose I will," he agreed, eyes remaining on the phantoms.

Alaric looked past James to Tallie, Alejandro, and Damon on the hill. They knew they were likely on a suicide mission from the start. If they tried to run now, Aislin would have them hunted and killed. If they tried to take Madeline by force, they would have to contend with an army of phantoms.

"Their choices are poor," Madeline commented, almost as if reading Alaric's mind.

He was used to her reading his emotions, but to pluck such a keen observation from emotions alone seemed far fetched at best. Perhaps she had not only gained an army, but a few new tricks as well.

She paused in thought, then said, "We cannot let them leave to spread word of what they've seen here. We can give them the choice to join us, but they cannot be set free."

James had finally braved the phantoms enough to stand near Alaric and Madeline. He lowered his voice as he commented, "If they join us, they're little more than mutineers."

Madeline smiled at him. "Aren't we all?"

James smirked. "I suppose we are, but the fact remains, they cannot be trusted. They might turn on you the moment you let down your guard."

Madeline laughed. "Then I will not let down my guard."

She walked forward, trailing her phantoms behind

her, leaving Alaric and James behind to gawk at her back. She reached the edge of the rocky beach then walked across the lush grass toward the waiting trio. Alejandro seemed hesitant to remain where he was, but Tallie and Damon stood strong.

"You have two options," Madeline called out as she neared them. "Accept a new queen, or die."

Alaric's heart dropped as Damon abruptly threw himself toward Madeline, a blade gleaming in his hand. Alaric began to rush forward, but there was no need. Before the blade could strike, three banshees dropped down in front of him, letting out horrid cries.

Damon skidded to a halt, gazing at the spectral women before him, awestruck. As Alaric reached Madeline's side, Damon began to sputter while clutching at his throat. His hands moved to claw at his face, eyes still intent on the banshees before him. Everyone watched in silent horror as he fell to his knees, then keeled over, dead. It had all happened so quickly Alaric felt frozen. He'd had no time to act, and wasn't even sure what he would have done if he had.

Tallie and Alejandro dropped to their knees before Madeline. Not looking up, Tallie explained, "Our job was never to bring you back with us. It was to kill you. Aislin did not believe the charm is within you, and wants you dead so she may claim it for herself."

Thoughts raced through Alaric's mind as he tried to ignore the dead man at their feet. It was Estus who wanted Madeline alive after all. Had Estus learned the charm was within Madeline, or did he simply understand he couldn't take it from her regardless? Still, Alaric wasn't sure how Estus would hope to use her. She was a force to be reckoned with, and held no love for the aged Doyen. After the scene with Damon, he did not envy Estus' chances at survival.

Madeline crouched and released the life from Damon's body, not bothering to even look down at him, then stood to face Alaric, ignoring Tallie and Alejandro.

Alaric still longed to hold her, but she was not *his* Madeline, not right now at least. He hated that his first thought was that maybe Mikael would know what to do, but he really was their best hope in that moment. The Viking had been alive over 1,300 years, and had acquired a great deal of arcane knowledge in that time.

Alaric knew he should be setting some sort of plan in motion, but he couldn't seem to fully focus on the details with Damon's dead body lying a few feet away. He wasn't bothered as much by the death, as Madeline's reaction to it. Madeline *always* cared about death. She valued the lives of heroes and villains alike.

Madeline seemed as if she were about to say something to him, but something else caught her attention. Alaric followed her gaze past the still waiting Tallie and Alejandro to two distant forms. Relief flooded through him. Mikael and Sophie.

He never thought he'd feel such happiness to see someone he utterly detested, but there it was. He was at a complete loss with Madeline, sensing that if he pointed out that she was being influenced into decisions that weren't her own, she'd simply leave. Whatever foreign energies were inside her likely held no love for him, so if the part of Madeline that was still Madeline wasn't strong enough, he didn't stand a chance.

Mikael and Sophie broke into a jog upon seeing them. Both wore modern clothing that would have blended in anywhere. Sophie's of course, was uniform black.

Neither hesitated at the sight of the phantoms still swirling around Madeline, though Sophie did watch them warily as they approached.

Tallie turned to their new company, then took a step back. "You're Mikael," she gasped. She turned back to Alaric. "You had planned to ambush us from the start," she accused, then quickly went pale as one of the phantoms darted a little too close to her, blowing her hair away from her face with the sudden gust.

Mikael stepped forward. "On the contrary." He winked at Tallie, then walked past her. "We caught word from my contacts on this continent of one of the Vaettir, a woman, raising the spirits of the restless dead across the countryside, paying little heed to any who might witness the odd sight." His eyes focused on Madeline. "Some of them were nearby, trying to figure out a way to kill you before I intervened. At that time, Sophie caught wind of her brother, leading us here."

Madeline's smile sent a chill down Alaric's spine. "Kill me?" she laughed. "Let them try."

Mikael's expression didn't change, though there was a certain wariness in his gaze. "There will be no need for that. Save your strength for our enemies."

Madeline smiled even wider. "If I expend my strength, I will simply gather more." She turned back to Alaric. "We've waisted enough time. We must choose the location of the final battle."

"We need to stop and think," he cautioned. There had to be a way to reach the *real* Madeline, to pull her back from the abyss.

James grunted in agreement, reminding Alaric that he was right beside him. He'd been so distracted that he'd forgotten his once friend, now long-time enemy had been there at all.

"I've made my choice," Madeline said evenly.

She turned away from Alaric to regard Tallie and Alejandro, both of whom went green with the new attention. "Send word to Aislin. I will await her on the battlefield, but tell her nothing else. If you betray me, I promise your deaths will be much worse than your Doyen could ever manage."

Before Alaric could reach out and grab her, the phantoms lifted Madeline back into the air. She didn't look at him at all as she was carried away, back toward the coast. Within moments, she faded from view, almost as if she'd been absorbed into the swirling fog composed of spirits.

Mikael closed the final distance between them with Sophie following shortly behind. His long, auburn hair blew back from his face as a particularly harsh, cold breeze came in from the coast.

The breeze prickled Alaric's skin with electricity, as if it carried unnatural energy with it.

Mikael glanced between Alaric and Sophie. "*That* was not Madeline."

Alaric turned away from Mikael and his sister to gaze off in the direction Madeline had gone. "At first I thought the key had taken her over again," he explained, "but there's something more. I believe the Morrigan has shielded herself inside her as well. They all now work toward the same purpose."

Alaric turned back to Mikael to find that he had been gazing at the coast with him.

Swallowing his pride, Alaric asked, "How do we fix this?"

Mikael shook his head. "We summoned a deity to *fix* this, and we've only succeeded in making things worse. I do not know how to fix this."

Alaric felt like he wanted to scream, to curse the entire planet for providing the one he loved with such a tumultuous existence. He couldn't lose her and their child now. He had promised to protect them both.

"We have to try," he urged, willing the Viking to agree with him.

If Mikael gave up, Alaric would force Tallie to find Madeline again. He did not know what he'd do when he found her, but he couldn't *not* find her.

"I swore an oath to her," Mikael said coldly, seeming

to sense what Alaric was thinking. "Despite what you may think of me, I hold true to my oaths."

Alaric breathed a sigh of relief, then gestured back to the waiting Tallie and Alejandro. "Tallie can find her, given enough time," he explained. "We just need to wait until Madeline remains in one place long enough for a perceptible amount of energy to build."

Mikael glanced back at Tallie, then turned away, seeming to dismiss her. "We cannot remain one step behind. We must anticipate Madeline's next move."

He clenched his fists. "No one could have anticipated any of this."

"She's going to gather more power," Mikael observed, not offended by Alaric's tone. "She wants a *final battle*, but which part of her wants it? The key would be motivated toward that goal. I don't see what the Morrigan would have to gain, but perhaps she would as well."

"What's your point?" Sophie growled, finally interjecting herself into the discussion.

Mikael shrugged. "I'm just trying to determine where Madeline is coming from. *Why* she has embarked on this endeavor."

"She's obviously been taken over by more powerful forces," Sophie grumbled. "Madeline is coming from nowhere. It's the key's actions we must predict."

Mikael shrugged again, but said nothing.

Sophie sighed. "What is it?" she asked tiredly. "What are you not saying?"

Mikael frowned. "I'm saying that the Morrigan and

the key might both want the final battle, but Madeline might want it too. Was her original intent not to use the deaths from a large battle to destroy the key?"

"I don't think Madeline is willingly going along with this," Alaric countered. "It's not something she would do just to beat the key. The last time she raised the dead . . . " he trailed off, thinking of Diana. "She was horrified. You saw those *things* she summoned. That is *not* her."

Mikael snorted. "I think you give her too little credit."

"On the contrary," Alaric argued, "I give her the credit she deserves. Madeline would not be reckless enough, and selfish enough to summon an army of spirits just for a chance to rid herself of the key."

Mikael smiled. "Unless she truly thinks she can win."

Alaric shook his head at Mikael's foolishness, then looked back to Tallie and Alejandro. They could have tried to run during their discussion, but hadn't. Of course, they had nowhere to go. If they didn't return with news that Madeline was dead soon, Aislin would send others to hunt them.

James walked forward, encompassing Tallie and Alejandro in the span of his gaze. "I chose the side I think most likely to win," he explained to them. "Will you do the same, or will you ride Aislin's sinking ship to your deaths, which will probably happen tomorrow?"

Tallie stood tall and unyielding. "I can find Madeline again, given the time. I've weighed the odds, and think this route my most likely chance of survival, but I want a guarantee of protection from Aislin."

She'd looked to Mikael as she'd said the last, and he nodded in reply.

Alejandro stepped up beside her, though he didn't seem happy about it, especially since Damon's corpse was only a few feet away. "I have no desire to go near the Phantom Queen again, but I will fight for the side not planning on sending assassins after me."

Alaric shivered. *Phantom Queen*. It sounded familiar to him.

"They called the Morrigan the Phantom Queen," Mikael observed, "not long before she left this world."

Alaric crossed his arms against the cold seeping into his bones. He was rarely affected by cold, but he was sure feeling it now.

"There is a Salr here," Alaric explained to Mikael and Sophie. "We can wait until Tallie gets a sense of where Madeline is. Perhaps she'll even come back."

"I will send for my people to gather on this continent," Mikael replied, turning his gaze back to the coast. "We must be ready, should Madeline spring the *final* battle on us." His expression turned pensive. "I must speak to my contacts once more to see if they can grant me any further insight into what Madeline has done."

Before Alaric could accuse him of planning to run off, Mikael met his eyes firmly and said, "I will keep my oath to her."

Alaric sealed his lips into a tight line and nodded. "As will I."

The two men turned away from each other, Alaric

marching in the direction of the Salr with the rest of their party following, while Mikael walked off alone.

The only other oaths Alaric had ever sworn were to protect his sister, and to kill Mikael to avenge his mother. This latest oath, to save Madeline and his child, would have to take precedence. He'd waited hundreds of years to kill Mikael, but it no longer mattered. He was now only concerned with who needed to live, not who needed to die. Death could come later.

They were going to have a daughter, Madeline had said, and no ancient Viking, nor vengeful deity could compare to the importance of that.

13

Mikael had lied when he said he was going to meet with his contacts once more. He'd already learned all he could from them, and what they suspected regarding Madeline's whereabouts.

Madeline had spent the previous evening visiting ancient graveyards, many of which could not be found on any map. Some were mass graves of victims who'd suffered ill fates due to famine and war. Others were simply old. They were places where the spirits didn't truly rest, unwilling to let go of their natural lives.

Given her chosen locations, Mikael's contacts had speculated on where she might go next, and he had to agree with them.

There was a well known sight in Dublin called Bully's Acre. Originally a priory, hundreds of thousands of people had been buried in the area, starting as early as the 1170s. The gravesite had eventually been leveled, leaving no record of most of the bodies beneath the earth. It was a perfect place for Madeline to fill out her ranks, with so many dead in one space.

He found the odds especially likely, since she had covered most of Northern Ireland during the previous night. It would only make sense for her to cover the South before moving on to other continents, if she moved on at all. Ireland was the Morrigan's chosen homeland, so it figured her phantoms would come from there, and only there.

Madeline had proven she could cover many graveyards in a single evening, and Bully's Acre would undoubtedly be on her list. So that was where Mikael would head, on his own. He knew Alaric would not forgive him for omitting him from his plans, but he also knew he could not take him. Madeline was not herself. If she harmed Alaric while possessed, it would kill her later. Mikael's only hope was their blood oath. If Madeline caused him harm, the earth would come to claim her. With any luck, he would have a chance to remind her of that fact before she killed him.

If it was in both the Morrigan's and the key's best interest to keep Madeline alive, they would at the very least exercise caution, or so he kept telling himself. In reality, any positive outcome would require a great deal of luck. He'd always been lucky, but this was pushing it.

Still, he didn't think twice before climbing into the car he and Sophie had driven to the countryside. He never reconsidered as he took the narrow country road toward the highway.

Dublin was several hours away, but it was barely midday. Madeline had visited the other graves under the cover of night, so it would stand to reason that if she did indeed visit Bully's Acre, it would not be until the sun went down. He had time.

Even so, as soon as he reached the end of the country road and turned onto the highway that would take him South, he sped down it like a bat out of hell. Once he reached an area where his cell had service, he called Aila, instructing her and Faas to catch the next flight to Ireland, leaving Tabitha to gather the rest of his people, urging them out of hiding.

Faas would not appreciate being separated from his sister, but he would be needed to determine just what was going on inside Madeline. Since he could drain and analyze the spiritual energy from others, he'd be able to tell Mikael just how much space the Morrigan and the key were now taking up . . . if Madeline didn't kill him first.

The key would most definitely see Faas as a threat, since Faas could weaken its vessel. The real Madeline would willingly let Faas take her energy. The other energies, most likely, would put up a fight.

He clenched his jaw and focused on the road. After all he had sacrificed, all he had lost, he would not lose to the key now. This was a battle begun long before Madeline was born, and he would see it through to the bitter end.

"YOU SHOULDN'T HAVE LET Mikael go," James argued as soon as they were back within the Salr.

"He won't harm Madeline, " Alaric sighed, scenting the air for Kira.

He knew he had already gotten all of the information out of her that he could, but he couldn't just sit and wait for Tallie to sense the key. He *had* to act. If Kira couldn't be found, he would read the Morrigan's books cover to cover, despite the language barrier. Perhaps their pages held some way to reverse what had been done to Madeline. If so, he'd do his best to decipher it.

"How can you be so sure?" James asked, following Alaric down the narrow hall.

Tallie and Alejandro had gone ahead, claiming a room to get some rest after disposing of Damon's body. Alaric probably should have gotten some rest himself, but even after not sleeping the previous night, he knew any efforts he made would be fruitless. There was no way he could sleep so soon after losing Maddy once again.

He had no answer for James, or rather, none he was willing to give. He sensed Mikael was either in love with Madeline, or he'd found some other sort of camaraderie within her that Alaric didn't quite understand. Either way, the Viking was intent on rescuing her. Mikael might betray Alaric and James, but he would not betray Madeline, even if there wasn't an oath holding him in line.

He decided to give up on his search for Kira, since James would probably pester him the entire way. Instead, he stopped at the room containing the Morrigan's books.

"You didn't answer me," James said evenly, following him in.

"He swore a blood oath to Madeline," Alaric explained. "You were there, if you recall."

James snorted. "All of that time seems like a dream to me."

Alaric lifted one of the heavy tomes from the table and slumped into a chair to peruse its contents. "It was more like a nightmare, seeing you cower in fear with only the slightest provocation."

"Yeah," James grumbled. "You must have *loved* seeing that."

"I'd rather not see you at all," Alaric replied simply.

He knew he was baiting James, but he was itching for a fight. Too much inaction and too much fear over Madeline's predicament left him grasping for something to focus his attention on. Why did James even want to converse with him in the first place?

James picked up a book himself, not really looking at it. "You say that," he argued, "but then why am I still here, and not in an unmarked grave with Diana?"

Alaric shrugged and focused on the book, not

wanting to put Sophie in the spotlight. She was off exploring the rest of the new Salr on her own, and she'd not thank him for giving away her secret to James.

"Answer me," James demanded, raking his hands through his golden hair with an irritated flick.

Alaric glared at him. "We considered leaving you unconscious, but didn't want you relaying any information to Aislin."

"*And*?" James pressed.

Alaric shrugged again, giving in if it meant James would leave him alone. "And my sister didn't have the heart to kill a man while he was unable to defend himself. Sophie has never been much of a killer."

James smirked. "If she was, I'd be dead ten times over, though I'm not sure why you've never tried to do it for her."

Alaric looked back down at his book. "Sophie can fight her battles as she chooses."

"And Madeline?" James walked to the front of the empty fireplace, his back to Alaric. "Can *she* fight her battles as she chooses?"

Alaric frowned behind James' back. "If Madeline were in her right mind, I would respect her decisions. I *have* respected her decisions thus far. Yet I will not stand idly by while foreign energies use her body for their own purposes."

"And you're so sure that Madeline has no control in this situation?"

Unable to focus on reading, Alaric put down his

book. "You saw the same display as I. We both know Madeline would never speak like that. She would never have brushed off Damon's death so easily."

"Or maybe the little mouse is growing fangs," James taunted, turning away from the fireplace to face him, "and you're worried that they'll be bigger than yours."

Alaric raised an eyebrow at him. "You truly think that was Madeline speaking, and not the key or the Morrigan?"

James smirked again. "She was looking at you with the same sappy eyes she always does. *That* look didn't come from the key, and I doubt it came from the Morrigan, given how she feels about men. Madeline might not have been pulling all the strings, but my guess is she's a willing partner in this endeavor, not a prisoner." He turned back to the empty fireplace and began stacking some nearby logs in the center.

Alaric shook his head, turning his attention back to the book. The Madeline he knew would never summon a phantom army. Of course, the Madeline he first met would not have made it this far to begin with. Maybe he wasn't giving her enough credit. Or, perhaps he was giving her *too* much credit by assuming she'd take the moral high ground, despite the consequences. Perhaps Madeline was more like the other Vaettir than he'd originally thought.

He wasn't sure if it was a comforting thought, or a frightening one. On one hand, a callous outlook bettered her chances of survival. On the other, it changed who she was. Madeline's unyielding respect for life was a part of her. It had shaped who she was, and in many ways, it had shaped him during the time that he'd spent with her. He didn't want her to change, and he wasn't sure if his concern was for her, or for himself.

That thought alone troubled him. He wasn't used to the dynamics of a committed relationship, and he wasn't sure how selfless or selfish he was supposed to be.

He pushed his thoughts away as he read the text in front of him. None of it mattered, really, since as far as the odds were concerned, neither of them would survive very long.

Forget phantoms, deities, and the key. A battle between the two largest clans of the Vaettir would mean bloodshed like their race had never seen, and it would undoubtedly spill over into the human world. There was no way to contain it.

Even if they lived, their lives would be changed forever. There was no telling in what way, but he was quite sure it wouldn't be good.

His attention was brought back to James as the fire roared to life. He looked a question at him as he rose, surprised that James would be considerate enough to build a fire.

Not meeting Alaric's eyes, James muttered, "I'm going to get some rest. I suggest you do the same."

Alaric nodded as James left him, turning his eyes back to the book. There was an image of a woman sacrificing a man before him. The accompanying chant called to death and darkness for power.

Though Madeline could bring death, that wasn't all she was. She was *light* and compassion. She wouldn't take part in a ritual that worshipped only death.

Would she?

14

Mikael walked amongst the gravestones dotting the grassy earth like the broken teeth of some long-dead giant. He thought he could almost *feel* the energy of the dead below, but it was probably just paranoia. Sensing the dead, or energies in general, was not one of his talents.

The sun was yet to set, so a few humans, tourists most likely, milled about the ancient gravesite. There weren't many since the winter months weren't the tourist high season. Hopefully they would leave before full dark. Witnessing what Madeline had to offer might be a bit more than the visitors had bargained for on their trip to Ireland.

He took a seat on a nearby bench to wait, fidgeting nervously. It wasn't often that his nerves got the better of him, but it also wasn't often he went into a situation he was unlikely to win. Best case scenario, Madeline would hop a ride with her phantoms to get away from him. Worst case, she would disregard her oath and kill him, then the earth would claim her in turn. Of course, there was a third option. She might gather enough power to find a way around their oath, and would kill him with no consequences.

He could only hope enough of the real Madeline was still beneath the surface to not want to hurt him. Of course, if the key was in control, it might not kill him either. The key would use anyone it could, and Mikael was rather useful. However, if the Morrigan was in charge, he would die. He trusted that witch even less than he trusted the key.

He remained on his bench as darkness slowly crept across the countryside, chasing away the humans visiting the historical site. He felt more comfortable as the last of the visitors left, then grimaced at the thought of what might have happened had Madeline shown up with her phantoms in public.

Mikael wasn't worried about what the humans would think. Most humans wouldn't believe the story of a ghost army descending upon an ancient graveyard. It would be passed off as poisonous gasses seeping up from the ground to make people hallucinate, or some other such rationalization. He was more worried about the idea of Madeline harming people. Her conscience would destroy her in the end, if they ever managed to restore her to her original self at all.

As full darkness fell, he continued to wait, but there

was no sign of Madeline. He decided to move to a less conspicuous spot, not only worried a security guard might approach, but also not wanting Madeline to see him first. If she saw him first, she might simply flee.

His mind made up, he moved silently to a more secluded area of the gravesite and crouched in the darkness, where he continued to wait.

The hours crept on. He'd left his cell phone in the rental car, and had no watch to tell the time, but he guessed it was somewhere around midnight. He cursed silently. He'd been so sure Madeline would want to utilize Bully's Acre, but perhaps he was wrong. Perhaps she went to another continent entirely, and he had no hope of finding her without Tallie's help.

Still, he would wait the night out in the graveyard, just in case. He pushed his hair back away from his face as a cool breeze hit him, sending goosebumps up and down his arms. Normally he was fairly tolerant to the cold, but there was something about this breeze that wasn't quite right. It felt like it was laced with electricity, yet there was no storm to provide lightning.

He continued to crouch as he heard light footsteps on the grass not far off.

"I didn't expect to find you hiding in a graveyard," a voice said, suddenly near him.

He rose abruptly and turned toward the voice. Madeline stood roughly twenty feet away, alone. At least, she appeared to be alone. Mikael had little doubt the phantoms could swoop in without a moment's notice.

He took a step toward her. "Well you left so suddenly this morning, we never got to finish our conversation."

Madeline closed the distance between them. Over her sweater and jean ensemble, she'd added a knee-length, black coat that billowed around her legs as she moved, adding to the *Phantom Queen* imagery quite nicely. Her long, wavy hair danced around her shoulders and waist as the breeze played with the loose tendrils. Standing before him, she turned her face upward, her expression calm.

Looking down at her smaller form, Mikael could have sworn she was the normal Madeline. The look in her pale blue eyes was familiar, unlike the presence of a foreign power.

"It really is you in there, isn't it?" he observed.

"Did you doubt it?" she asked, sounding like Madeline, only slightly off. He realized with a start that the new tone in her voice was confidence.

"But there are others inside of you as well . . . " he trailed off, feeling the urge to reach out and touch her to verify she was real.

She nodded, sending her hair forward over her shoulders. "You were already aware of the presence of the key. Now the Morrigan helps us too."

He sighed. He didn't want to contradict Madeline out of fear she'd take off again, but he also wanted to keep their civil conversation going. "Up until now, I was under the impression we were fighting *against* the key."

Madeline tilted her head to the side in thought, a

very un-Madeline gesture. "For now, our purpose is the same. We must work together to achieve our goals. Once our enemies have been dealt with, the key and I can have a stand off of our own."

Mikael nodded, outwardly accepting her answer, even though he didn't accept it at all. "If we are to defeat our enemies, it would be nice to have you around to plan with us."

Madeline frowned. "I must finish summoning my army first."

His palms began to sweat. Something about the whole conversation was unnerving. He remembered when Erykah had been tied to the key. Sometimes it spoke through her, but not like this. This was like Madeline's personality had actually melded with the other forces.

"You're nervous," Madeline observed. "That's new."

Mikael was momentarily shocked that he'd let his mental shields down, or had he? His eyes widened slightly as he focused his attention inward. His shields were still firmly in place. Her empathic powers must have increased along with everything else.

"Can you blame me?" he asked.

She shook her head and smiled. "No, I don't blame you, but I must ask you to stand aside while I retrieve what I came here for."

Ignoring her request, Mikael asked. "Is it *you* that wants this, or is it the Morrigan?"

Madeline laughed, surprising him. "You all think I'm

so weak. The Morrigan saw my strength. She knew I could do this on my own."

Mikael laughed in reply. "If I thought you were weak, I would never have allied myself with you to begin with. Our oath goes both ways, so you know I'm not lying."

That seemed to give Madeline pause. "If that is the case, then you can trust that I know what I'm doing."

"I do trust you," he replied. "I just want to make sure that this is *your* choice."

"It is, now please stand back."

"At least come reassure Alaric that you and your child are both okay!" he blurted out as she began to slowly raise her arms. "This uncertainty is killing him."

Her intent expression faltered, once again giving Mikael hope the real Madeline was reachable.

"I'm doing this for both of them," she replied. "This is the only chance we have to all survive."

"Then come back to the Salr and tell him that," Mikael urged.

He really didn't care about Alaric's well-being, and Madeline probably sensed that, but it was still something *she* would care about, or at least, the real Madeline would.

"I can't," she stated. "We're running out of time, and the banshees are growing restless."

Mikael shivered at the mention of banshees. He'd been alive when banshees still roamed the countryside, and had no desire to go up against one.

Madeline shut her eyes, as if trying to shut something out. She was beginning to seem panicked, letting Mikael know that he was running out of time himself. He couldn't let her flee.

"I need to remind you of something," he said calmly. "*All* of you," he added, including the key and the Morrigan in his statement.

Madeline turned suddenly bored eyes to him, like she had once again been taken over by the calm, confident energy.

"Madeline," he began slowly, putting emphasis on her name, "you and I have an oath. If you directly harm me, or if you order anyone, or *anything* else to harm me, the earth will claim you. Your mortal form will cease to be, and therefore the key, and perhaps even the Morrigan, will cease to be."

Madeline was so still, he couldn't even tell if she was breathing. He knew he had to act fast, otherwise the banshees would come and take her away.

He darted forward and scooped her up in his arms. The moment he touched her, the banshees darted down from the sky, letting out ear-piercing shrieks.

Mikael ran forward, throwing Madeline over his shoulders, holding on tight. The banshees swarmed them, but caused no harm. What he'd said about the oath must have worked. Whoever controlled the banshees also knew that harming Mikael with Madeline's powers or her army would break her oath, and hence end Madeline. It would all be over if Madeline no longer existed.

Darting through the cemetery, he tightened his grip on the back of her thighs, hoping she wouldn't view this kidnapping as a form of betrayal. He was also saving her, was he not? If he did not try to save her, would that not also be a form of betrayal? He was taking a risk, but saw no other choice.

He spotted the rental car ahead. Madeline hadn't fought back, she might yet as she hadn't had much time to react. When she did, she might reason that she could harm him without breaking their oath, as she'd just be defending herself. Reaching the car, he flung open the driver's side door, set her in, then quickly lifted her over the center console to the passenger seat. He slid in after her and slammed the door shut, then started the car to peel away before Madeline had time to rebel.

"What the hell do you think you're doing!" she shouted as she recovered.

Mikael tore out onto the empty, night-time street.

"Saving you from yourself," he replied calmly, keeping his eyes on the road.

"You can't betray me like this!" she shouted. "Our oath prevents it!"

He smiled. If it was a betrayal, he would be dead right now. "Saving you from yourself is not a betrayal. Allowing you to be controlled by other beings *is*."

"You're afraid," she spat back. "I can feel fear wafting from you like foul perfume."

He clenched his jaw. "I just kidnapped the *Phantom Queen*, not entirely knowing if doing so would break my oath and thus, would quickly end my life. Of course I'm afraid."

Madeline quieted at that. Her sudden shift in demeanor was unnerving. "Well you've stopped me from my task, for now, so what do you want? You can't keep me indefinitely. There are too many things in motion now."

His foot pressed more firmly on the gas pedal. "I just wanted to talk with you without the risk of you getting angry and running away."

He couldn't bring her back to the Salr where Alaric and the others waited. Not yet. Still, he needed to take her somewhere the banshees couldn't reach them.

"So talk," she demanded. "I've got things to do."

Talking in the car was really probably as good a place as any. As long as they were moving, it would be difficult for her to escape.

"What happened with the Morrigan?" he asked, wanting the specifics of what was going on before he addressed any further issues.

Madeline sighed. "Why should I tell you?"

Mikael grunted in annoyance, flexing his fingers on the steering wheel. "Perhaps because we're friends. Or because we've been helping each other since this all began. If not for those reasons, let's go with the fact that I've saved your ass plenty of times, and you owe me."

Madeline was silent for several minutes, then finally answered, "She killed herself, at least in part, to summon the banshees. A portion of her energy is inside me now, so I can bring her back."

"How?" Mikael demanded, hating the idea that the Morrigan had become a part of Madeline, almost as much as he hated the key being a part of her. "How will you bring her back?" he clarified.

Madeline was silent again, then answered. "I don't know. I imagine she'll tell me when it's time."

Mikael frowned. "And the key?" he pressed. "You're now working with it, rather than against it?"

Out of the corner of his eye, he saw her shrug. "For now we all share the same goal. Any conflicts will be addressed after that goal has been met."

"After we destroy our enemies?" Mikael asked, then added, "Are you even thinking about the fallout of such a large scale battle? Don't get me wrong, I agree that it must happen, but it will change the world forever. There is no way to hide such a thing from the humans. Many lives will be lost after the fact. Everything will be out of balance. Are you willing to shoulder the consequences of that?"

"Our plan is to restore balance," she said immediately, then turned pleading eyes to him. "Don't you see?"

Glancing at her, he slowed down briefly to take a turn, then sped back up. There was still no sign of banshee pursuit. Perhaps Madeline had ordered them to fall back.

"I'll see if you tell me," he replied.

He fully understood that small actions could have

very long term consequences. He'd been around long enough to see things that had happened a thousand years prior affect the present day. Things that had happened to *him* a thousand years prior.

"I can't," she replied softly. "You're just going to have to trust me."

He was surprised to realize that he *did* trust her, as he trusted very few people on this earth. Still, he didn't trust the warring forces inside her.

"I trust *you*," he replied, hoping she would get why he was putting emphasis on the *you*.

She was staring at him so intently, he glanced away from the road again.

"I'm not a slave, or merely a vehicle in this situation," she said evenly, meeting his gaze.

Her eyes were so intense, Mikael wondered if she was trying to tell him more than she was saying.

He turned his gaze back to the road with a sigh. "I can see that. I just hope you can tell the difference between your thoughts and the *others*."

Mikael glanced at her again, catching a brief glimpse of worry before she wiped it away.

"Where are we going?" she demanded.

"Where do you want to go?"

She snorted. "I already went to where I needed to go, and you took me away."

"I asked where you *wanted* to go," he countered, "not where you needed to go."

When she didn't reply, he added, "You really should

speak to Alaric. Assure him you're okay. He'll never believe it coming from me."

He glanced at her raising an eyebrow at him, her pale blue eyes soft. "So you believe that I'm okay?"

"I believe that you're strong enough to get through this," he replied evenly, "and lucky enough to perhaps come out alive. I believe fate has chosen you for this role, so as much as I'd like to fight it, I cannot."

"You've always struck me more as an *I make my own fate* kind of guy."

Mikael smirked. "In many ways yes, but far too much has happened for me to consider it mere happenstance. That the key would fall into the hands of a descendant of the Morrigan herself, that *has* to be fate."

She turned her gaze away from him to look out the passenger window. "I can't see Alaric," she said softly.

"Why?" he demanded.

Mikael hated that he was defending the man, but he really did believe it was in Madeline's best interests to be around him if she wanted to maintain the part of herself that was *her*.

She continued to gaze out the window, partially turned away from him. "I think you of all people can understand that he would distract me from what I need to do. If I'm with him, and we begin to think about our child, our *daughter*, I'll just want to run away and hide from everything to keep them safe. I can't do that. I have to be brave."

"That's one way to look at it," Mikael began, "*or* you

could draw strength from him. There's nothing wrong with accepting help."

"I don't need it," she snapped, suddenly defensive, though Mikael sensed it was still Madeline talking, and Madeline who'd somehow been offended by what he'd said.

A thought dawned on him. Madeline's drastic attitude change could have been a defensive reaction to the Morrigan manipulating her. He fully understood the intricacies of manipulation. He was the descendant of Dolos after all.

"She made you feel weak, didn't she?" he asked before he could think better of it. The Morrigan was still inside Madeline, after all, but Madeline seemed to be the one doing the talking at the moment.

Madeline glared at him. "Perhaps at first. Then she showed me how strong I really am."

"It takes just as much strength to accept help as it does to do things on your own," he countered.

Madeline nodded. "Yes, but there is a difference between accepting someone's protection, and *needing* it."

He sighed. "You've come far from the Madeline I knew."

He'd meant it in part as a compliment, but Madeline obviously didn't take it that way.

"The Madeline you knew was weak," she snapped.

"The Madeline I knew made a promise to my wife," he snapped back, finally getting angry. Had she forgotten everything?

She seemed taken aback. "You're really just going to have to trust me," she said finally.

By her tone, he felt again she was trying to tell him more than she was saying. Was she perhaps shielding certain thoughts from the key, and thus unable to voice her true plans out loud?

"I'll trust you if you come back to the Salr with me," he offered, hoping he wasn't making the wrong decision.

Madeline sighed. "Fine, but I won't stay. I can't lose any more time."

He nodded. "Talk to Alaric, then we'll stand back while you do whatever you need to do."

Madeline went silent after that.

He took the turn that would lead them back toward the Salr. There was still no sign of any banshees. He almost wanted to ask Madeline if she was keeping them at bay, but he couldn't quite bring himself to do it. He wasn't sure if it was more frightening that she had control over things straight out of men's nightmares, or if she didn't. One option made Madeline a huge force to reckon with all on her own, and the other meant that they were all completely screwed.

15

My pulse picked up speed as the car slowed, then came to a stop. We'd driven as far as we could toward the Salr, and would have to walk the rest of the way. It would be dawn soon, meaning I had lost an entire night of progress, but that wasn't what had me frightened.

It had been hard enough for me to leave Alaric the first time. I wasn't sure if I could do it again. I wasn't sure if I could look away from the option of having him embrace me. To *protect* me.

Yet, I knew what I had to do. No one could help me with the task before me. If I wasn't strong enough to do it, then no one could save me regardless.

I startled when a blast of cold air hit me. The passenger car door was open, revealing Mikael. I'd been so absorbed in my thoughts I hadn't realized he'd exited the car. He stood there, leaning toward me, offering a hand to help me out, a much more polite gesture than when I'd been forced in. I took his hand and slid out of the car. Fatigue washed over me, more than I'd felt in days.

With a start, I realized I'd now gone two entire nights without sleep, though the entire span of time seemed like a blurry dream. I needed rest. I had to keep my strength up if I hoped to not only survive, but to maintain my identity against the powerful forces within me.

Releasing my hand without a word, Mikael led the way toward the Salr. I followed, wrapping my coat tightly around myself in an attempt to shut out the freezing cold coastal wind. It was of little use. When I'd been among the banshees, I had barely felt the cold. Now without their presence, I felt human again. Weak and fragile.

The thought was almost enough for me to summon them forward. I had pushed them away once I'd arrived at Bully's Acre, not wanting to make a scene with any humans that might be hanging around the historical site late at night. My foresight had been to my detriment, since it had allowed Mikael time to grab me before the banshees could. Once I'd been thrown into the car, it only took a single thought to hold them back again. I'd known deep inside that this meeting was something I couldn't avoid, though it scared me half to death.

As I walked, I pictured Alaric's face when I told him he couldn't help me. He'd gone through hell for me, and had put me through a bit of hell himself. Still, I couldn't deny the fact that he'd proven his love, even if it was a love I didn't fully understand.

I'd thought what I'd experienced with Matthew, my first real boyfriend, had been love, especially after I'd accidentally released his life, but I'd been wrong. I knew now what love felt like. I knew what it was like to sit next to someone and feel utterly at home. I didn't know why that love had come so suddenly, and I could speculate until the cows came home whether it was fate, or just that Alaric and I had similar natures that drew us together, but it didn't really matter. What mattered was that it was there, and there was no arguing with it . . . though I was about to try.

I unwrapped my arms from myself to rub the small bump of my belly as Mikael walked silently beside me in the darkness. Alaric wouldn't understand, but I was doing this as much for him as I was for myself and our daughter.

Eventually, we reached the circle of rocks leading to the Salr. There was no one there to greet us, not that I expected there to be. Mikael wasn't one to share his plans unless he thought it absolutely necessary.

He crouched and touched a small stone on the ground to trigger the entrance. The action would only work for one of the Vaettir, a little quirk possessed by every Salr. I clutched at my belly again, not wanting to descend into the earth, even as we began to sink.

Mikael gave me an encouraging smile in the moon-light, then suddenly we were underground. I turned to glance down the familiar hallway, expecting to see Alaric waiting right there, but he wasn't.

The person I did see was the woman, one of Aislin's people, who'd been with Alaric when I'd arrived at the Salr the previous morning.

Her eyes widened as she saw me, then she averted her gaze and hurried down the hall until she was out of sight, her long, dark hair whipping behind her.

I turned to Mikael in surprise, then suddenly realized why she was afraid. My banshees had killed a man she knew right in front of her. I barely even remembered the scene, and that thought alone made me shiver. Maybe being around the energy of the phantoms had altered me more than I'd realized.

Mikael gestured for me to move forward, and I did, since the only other choice was climbing back out of the Salr.

I walked down the familiar hall, half expecting to walk around a corner and see Mara, even though there was no way for that to happen.

Not knowing where Alaric was, but somehow sensing where I should go, I approached the room where Mara and I had gone over her books. The door was slightly ajar.

I turned to look at Mikael for reassurance, but he'd stopped following me at some point. I was alone, and I'd been too absorbed to even notice his departure.

I took a deep breath and slowly pushed the door open. A fire had been made to dimly light the otherwise dark room. By its light, I could see Alaric's hunched form. He was leaning over the table, asleep on a pile of ancient books. His black hair hid his face from sight.

I approached him quietly, wanting desperately to see his face, though I was afraid to wake him. Unable to restrain myself, I gently pushed his hair back behind his ear.

Lightning fast, his hand shot up to grab my wrist. I let out a little yip of surprise, then relaxed as his eyes opened and focused on me.

Within seconds, he was up out of his chair, wrapping me in his embrace.

"I had the most terrible dream," he whispered into my hair.

I laughed softly, relieving some of my tension, if only temporarily. "It probably wasn't a dream."

He pulled back just enough to look into my eyes, though his arms remained around my waist, keeping me close.

"What made you come back?" he asked, suddenly very serious.

"Mikael," I admitted. "The man has a way with words, I'll give him that."

Alaric accepted my answer with a nod. I wanted nothing more than to kiss him in that moment, but I couldn't. I couldn't give in. Not yet.

His eyed me steadily. "Why do I have the feeling this is just a temporary reunion?"

I looked down, then forced myself to meet his eyes

again. The room was too hot with the fire and my coat, but I didn't want to pull away long enough to remove it.

"Because it is," I forced myself to say. "There are some things I need to do on my own."

"I can help you," he argued, anger in his tone. "We're in this together."

I shook my head and forced myself to pull away. "I just wanted to let you know that I'm okay, and that everything will make sense once the time comes."

Seeing that I wasn't coming back to his embrace, his arms dropped to his sides. "You seem different than you were the other morning," he commented, voice void of emotion, though what I was sensing from him was hitting me like a tidal wave.

"Being around that much power affected me more than I realized," I admitted. I slumped into one of the nearby seats, too tired to stand any longer.

Alaric resumed his seat next to me. The distance between us now felt like a dagger in my heart, but I couldn't pull it out.

"Yet you'll put yourself back in that position?" he asked.

"I have to," I answered immediately. "You don't understand what needs to be done."

"Then tell me."

"Not yet," I answered, urging him to understand.

I was shielding like a son of a bitch against the key. The Morrigan's energy was helping me, but we could only shield so much. Anything I said out loud would be clearly conveyed. The key shielded from us as well, so we had no idea how much it actually knew.

Alaric frowned. "At least stay here tonight. We can talk more about it in the morning."

I shook my head and looked down, fighting against the tears threatening to spill from my eyes.

"Have you eaten anything?" he asked, his voice suddenly cold.

I shook my head. "I need to go."

"You won't tell me what you plan, and you won't let me help you. The least you can do is let me feed you. You may have taken on extra power, but your body is still mortal, as is our child. You need to eat."

I nodded, suddenly feeling like a horrible person.

I thought he would leave the room to find food, but he only stood and went to a backpack I hadn't noticed previously, sitting in one of the chairs next to the fire.

He came back with two protein bars, an apple, a bag trail mix, and a bottle of water. He sat it all in front of me on the table, then resumed his seat.

My eyebrows raised as I looked down at the food. "Am I supposed to eat all of that?"

He nodded as I glanced over at him. "If you're only staying long enough to eat, then I'm going to feed you till you pop."

I smiled in spite of myself, glad for the excuse to stay, if only for a little while. I opened a protein bar. While I ate, Alaric took my free hand in his, watching me as if memorizing my every movement.

We gazed into each other's eyes often, as an unspoken agreement formed between us. He would trust while I climbed whatever mountains I needed, and would be there should I happen to fall.

"I'VE BEEN LOOKING for you everywhere," James said to Sophie, approaching her in the early morning light.

It was true. After speaking with Alaric, he'd gone to his room to rest. He'd fallen asleep only to wake in the wee hours of the morning with a single thought nagging at him. Why was he alive?

He didn't mean the thought in a existential sort of way. Instead, he just didn't understand why Sophie had insisted he come along after losing his memory. She'd been nothing but a bitch to him the entire time, yet here he was. He couldn't understand it, and he needed to know *why*.

Sophie turned, her face silhouetted by the barest hint of purple sunlight. He knew she'd smelled and heard him long before he reached her, but had only dignified him with acknowledgement once he'd made it clear he intended to speak with her.

She was just as beautiful as ever, and just as fierce, with her long, black hair framing her narrow, toned body, clad in black as usual. She leaned against a scraggly tree as if the weight of the world was pushing her down. Her ethereal features still took his breath away, just like always, though he'd never admit it now. She was the only girl he'd ever loved, and she'd torn his heart out.

"I have a question for you," he stated when she didn't speak.

"Go on," she said coldly.

"Why didn't you kill me? You've hated me since I killed Sammuel, and you had the perfect opportunity, so why didn't you kill me?"

She stared at him, and James suddenly felt like the vilest insect to have ever walked the face of the earth. She always made him feel like that. Like he wasn't worth nearly as much as she was.

"Well?" he growled, anger boiling in his stomach.

"I had just been left by Maya," she answered sadly, surprising him. "It left me feeling the slightest bit sentimental, but don't worry, it won't happen again."

He shook his head, tossing his golden hair forward to partially obscure his eyes. "I still don't get it. Don't you hate me?"

She turned away from him to gaze out at the slowly rising sun. "I hate you, and I always will. I can never forgive you. Don't get the wrong impression."

He took a step closer, wanting to reach out to her, but not wanting to lose a hand. "If your hatred is still that strong, then why not kill me?" he pressed, knowing he was taunting her, but unable to help himself.

Suddenly Sophie turned on him. "Because I'm not you!" she shouted. Her voice echoed across the land, carried far by the thin, morning air. In a more calm voice, she continued, "Just because I was betrayed by a monster, doesn't mean I have to become one."

James stepped back in shock. He didn't know what he'd expected, but it hadn't been *that*. All this time, he'd thought Sophie would enact her vengeance as soon as he gave her the chance, but in reality she'd never planned on it. She'd never planned on turning herself into exactly what he was. He realized with a start he'd been waiting around, hoping she would try. If she was just like him, then she couldn't hate him anymore.

He exhaled, suddenly feeling like he might just turn to dust to blow away on the breeze. He began to turn away, then mumbled, "You're a stronger person than I."

"What?" Sophie snapped, though James knew she'd heard him.

He turned to fully face her. "I thought you were a monster for leaving me for another man," he began, his anger threatening to spill over. His anger was always like that now, just below the surface, waiting to be unleashed. "So I became one in return," he continued. "I became a monster, because that's what I thought you were."

Sophie's eyes narrowed. "You were always a monster, James. I simply gave you to courage to be what you truly were."

James stared into her honest eyes, and couldn't quite handle what he saw there. It was easy to blame others for your actions. Accepting that you'd made your own choices was another thing entirely.

He turned abruptly and walked away, leaving Sophie to her thoughts.

Perhaps he *had* always been a monster. It didn't matter, as long as that's what he was now. Being a monster was a lot easier than feeling pain, and it was a hell of a lot less scary than experiencing heartbreak. Being a monster was the only thing that allowed him to walk away in that moment. It was the only thing that had allowed him to survive all this time around her. All this time being *hated* by her. A monster was all he would ever be, from that point forward.

He thought he heard Sophie crying as he walked away, but he shut the sound out. Monsters didn't care about the tears of others. They only cared about themselves.

"I HAVE TO GO," I argued, rising to my feet as Alaric held onto my hand.

I'd done my best to convince him, but it really was my fault as much as his that I hadn't left yet. The Morrigan's energy had started with subtle prodding, but her force had become almost overwhelming as I'd stalled the early morning away.

Alaric's face held so many unsaid things as his shoulders sagged in resignation. Suddenly he knelt in front of me, putting his face level with my belly.

To my surprise, he started speaking to it. "Now

daughter," he began, then smiled, still gazing at my stomach, "It feels very weird saying that, but I need you to listen." His eyes rolled up to me as he said the next part, "I trust your mother. I trust her not to listen to anyone's opinions but her own."

My breath caught. Did he understand? Did he know I could shield my thoughts from the key, but not my words?

He gave me solid eye contact as he continued, "I'll be counting the hours until I can see both of you again. All I need is the slightest sign, and I'll follow your mother to the ends of the earth. She and I will be together before you join us."

I held back tears as I used his hand to pull him to his feet. He hugged me hard enough it almost hurt, but I wouldn't have it any other way.

"I'll walk you out," he whispered in my ear.

I nodded, suddenly feeling afraid. Previously, I'd been so gung ho in my task, and so caught up in the energies that had surrounded me, I hadn't felt fear. It was all catching up with me now, but I knew what I needed to do. I would just have to be careful not to lose myself again.

We left the room and walked down the hall, hand in hand. I would have liked to thank Mikael, but I saw no sign of him, and I couldn't hold off the energies within me forever. I didn't want to risk riling them enough that they'd try to take over.

We reached the Salr's entrance with no obstacles, and ascended to the surface together.

Morning had come, the cheery sunlight contrasting with my mood. I heard footsteps and turned to see James stomping toward us, his energy chaotic. My attention was drawn away from him as the screech of a banshee sounded near the coast. As I watched, the phantoms sped toward me, even though I hadn't called for them. I'd kept them waiting too long, and they'd grown restless, ready to serve their purpose.

"I see you're both still pretending this can actually work out," James sniped.

Alaric and I turned back to see him scowling at our joined hands.

"I see you're still pretending we want to speak with you," Alaric replied coldly.

The banshees and other phantoms reached us, swirling around impatiently. Neither James nor Alaric seemed fazed, and I could sense some new tension between them that hadn't been there before.

I felt impatience welling up inside of me, but it wasn't mine. I was the opposite of impatient. I didn't want to go.

A wave of angry energy hit me, making me lose my grip on Alaric's hand. He snapped his head from James to me in surprise.

"I *felt* that," he gasped.

James' anger hit me a second later. I had no idea what he was so upset about, but I'd never felt his emotions like that. Usually, I hardly felt his emotions at all.

I looked at James in shock.

"Stop empathing me," he growled.

"I didn't mean—" I began, but was cut off as someone came into sight from the direction of the road. A moment later I realized it was Mikael, along with Aila and Faas, though I had no idea when the latter two had arrived.

Two of the banshees darted toward James, not liking the aim of his fury.

"Call them off," James demanded, his ire increasing.

"Maddy," Alaric said cautiously, grabbing my hand to give it a squeeze.

I closed my eyes and tried to let Alaric's calm seep in, but was met with the agitated energies of the key and the Morrigan. There was no calm to be found within me, and emotions were heightening all around me.

I sensed Sophie's approach without opening my eyes. She was angry, confused, and also scared. The more I sensed everyone's emotions, the more the feeling increased. I wasn't usually so easily overwhelmed, but my added power boost had increased my senses. It was becoming difficult to define where my feelings ended and everyone else's began.

Alaric was like a cool wind at my side, radiating calm because he knew that it helped me, but it wasn't enough.

The banshees darted at James again, trying to warn him away from me. I couldn't tell if they were being protective, or if they were just affected by his emotions as an extension of me.

"Stop it!" James shouted, not backing down, just as Mikael, Aila, and Faas reached us.

"You need to calm down," Faas said warily, looking at James, but James didn't seem to hear him.

James lashed out at the banshees whenever they came near, though mortal hands couldn't harm them. The only thing that could harm them was either someone who could control the dead, or who could control energy.

Suddenly panicked, I met Faas' eyes. "Don't," I said, "it will only make it worse."

His brow creased with worry, he nodded. If he tried to drain the energy from the banshees, it would only turn them toward attacking him instead.

I pulled away from Alaric and backed away from the group. It wasn't the goodbye I had in mind, but if I left, the banshees would leave with me.

Still, I felt like I was going to faint. The key's energy suddenly washed through me, awakened by the chaos of the moment.

"No," I breathed, a moment before I lost control.

My arm flung into the air, no longer controlled by my thoughts alone, sending the banshees forward. They swarmed their chosen target, James, knocking him to the ground. There was shouting all around, but I was too dizzy to make out what was happening.

I felt it the moment Faas began draining energy from

the banshees, but it was too late. There were too many of them.

"Focus on me," I screamed to Faas, knowing it was the only way to stop what was happening. Just as I gained energy from the banshees, they gained energy from me. Draining my power would weaken us all.

At first I didn't think Fass heard me, but a moment later I began to feel weak as my life force drained away. He was taking more energy than he ever had before, trying to stop what was happening to James. As he drained what felt like the last of *my* energy away, the Morrigan rushed forward, unwilling to give her power to anyone but me.

I felt a flying sensation, right before I lost consciousness. The last thing I heard was Alaric shouting my name.

16

I came to as we landed, realizing Mara had turned us into a crow, though I hadn't thought such a feat possible with my body as the host.

I lay face up in the grass, panting as a voice in my head explained, *Faas weakened us. I could not carry us far.*

Good, I thought in reply, wanting nothing more than to run back to make sure Alaric was okay. Now, if only I could stand.

"Hello Madeline," a voice said.

I held my breath in panic as I realized the voice wasn't *in* my head, but somewhere *near* my head. The panic wasn't from the innocuous greeting itself, but the person who'd given it. I recognized that eerily calm voice. A voice I'd never hoped to hear again.

"Estus," I breathed.

He came into view as he moved to stand over me. He was small, several inches shorter than me, but at the current angle he looked enormous. He smiled down at me, his lined face framed by his loose, silver hair flowing to his ankles.

"I've been searching for you," he explained, still smiling.

A voice in my head whispered, *Run*, but I still felt unable to stand. I reached out metaphysically, searching for the banshees, but nothing answered my call. I felt somehow blocked off.

Another person stepped into view, and if I had the energy, I would have screamed. *Aislin*.

At her side stood her executioner. The only time I'd ever seen him had been by the light of the moon. His hair had looked pure white then, and now that I could see it in the daylight, I could tell that it really was that white, though his angular face was young. His eyes looked gray or hazel, and held little emotion as he looked down at me.

"Marcos is a necromancer," Aislin explained, fluffing the full skirts of her ornate white dress around her. "He is blocking your phantoms from finding you, as well as the spirit that seems to have taken up residence within you."

She had to mean the Morrigan, and come to think of it, I could no longer sense her. I could still sense the key, but it wasn't offering me any help. I knew I should have been afraid, but my fear was secondary to a shocking realization that made sense of everything.

James and I had escaped from Estus' Salr so easily,

and Alaric had no trouble leaving to follow us. We'd found Diana, Aislin's sister, who led us right to the key. As much as we'd tried to create conflict between the two clans, they had continued to come after us, only attacking Mikael's people and not each other.

"You've both been working together all this time," I croaked, still feeling too weak to speak properly.

Aislin and Estus both smiled, while Marcos' face remained impassive.

"Clever girl," Aislin mocked. "You never stood a chance."

I glared at them. Even with the realization, I still had no idea *why* they were working together, or what they hoped to achieve if their goals weren't to defeat one another. Aislin had wanted me dead, her people had said so themselves, so why weren't they killing me now?

"The charm truly is inside her," Marcos remarked, "though I do not understand the other energy."

Aislin frowned. "I didn't think it possible. I thought for sure her man was lying. The charm never entered any of its previous hosts."

"What do you want?" I whispered, feeling like a lab specimen.

"We're going to save our race, my dear," Estus explained, "but first we need to find a way to separate you from the charm." He crouched down, putting his face inches from mine. "Even if it means we must cut you open to scrape it from your very soul."

I mustered what little strength I had left to scoot

away, wishing Faas hadn't drained me so violently. We hadn't flown far. Alaric and the others had to be somewhere near. There was still hope.

"Hope is a funny thing," Estus whispered, as if reading my mind. "It makes you strong in times of weakness, but leaves you when you truly need it most. This is a lesson you will learn very, very soon."

I struggled as Marcos crouched and lifted me up into his arms. I tried to lash out, to drain his energy, to do *something*, but he was like a brick wall to me. He began to carry me away, while I was still too weak to scream.

"They're gone," Aila panted, gazing up at the sky for any sign of the banshees.

They'd left moments after Madeline had gone. Alaric still couldn't quite believe what his eyes had shown him as Madeline fluidly shifted into the form of a crow. He'd seen the Morrigan do it, but had never guessed Madeline might be capable, even with the Morrigan's energy inside her.

Faas rose from his crouch, finished with releasing James' life. Madeline's abrupt departure had not come soon enough to save him.

Sophie now stood by Alaric, looking down at James' body with a strange expression. She leaned her head forward enough that her hair slithered over her shoulder to hide her face.

"I told him he was a monster," she muttered under her breath.

"He was," Alaric replied, not sure how to comfort his sister, if he should even comfort her at all. She might not need it, and she definitely wouldn't accept it.

Alaric looked up to Mikael, who stood by Aila. "How did you find her?" he asked. "She told me you were the one who brought her back here. So how did you find her?"

"Luck," Mikael grumbled, looking uncharacteristically angry. "That damn Morrigan. She's the cause of this. I know it. Madeline couldn't shift into a crow on her own. The Morrigan took over."

"Madeline was able to speak freely with me while we were in the Salr," Alaric explained, then backtracked, "As freely as she was able without giving anything away. I didn't get the feeling the Morrigan was who she was hiding things from."

Mikael frowned. "You noticed it too? Like she was afraid to say too much?"

"Or else the key might hear," Faas finished for them, quickly catching on to their train of thought.

Alaric turned back to his sister. "Go find Tallie. We need to know if she can sense anything."

Sophie didn't move. She just stared down at James.

"Sophie," Alaric demanded, "*go*."

She nodded a little too quickly, then left them to return to the Salr. Alaric knew Madeline had left in an attempt to call off the banshees, but something screamed in his mind that she wasn't safe. He felt a sense of urgency he couldn't quite explain. All he knew was that they needed to *act*. They could no longer wait.

Something green several miles off caught Alaric's eye. It was a darker green than the loamy ground, and sped toward them at an alarming speed.

"Kira," he observed as the tiny woman came fully into view.

She continued to run, impossibly fast like a bullet darting through the air, until she reached them and collapsed onto the ground at Alaric's feet.

"They took her!" she gasped, clutching at her throat for oxygen, her mishmash of bright clothing looking even more ridiculous in her current predicament.

She tossed her dark green hair out of her face, then began again, still panting, "Those people took Madeline. I wanted to help, but I thought I would help more by letting you know. You'll save her. You always do."

Kira's earnest eyes looked up into Alaric's, pleading.

"*Who* took her?" Alaric demanded, the screaming panic within him increasing tenfold.

"The old man and woman," Kira panted, "and the man with white hair. They said he was a necromancer."

Alaric was unsure what Kira meant by *the old man and woman*, but the white haired necromancer jogged something in his mind. Aislin's executioner had been white haired. Necromancy was a skill known to very few. It differed from the skills of an executioner on levels of control, but both were still similar in many ways. If

Aislin's executioner took Madeline, that had to mean that the old woman was Aislin, but then who was the old man? The only person who came to mind was Estus, but that didn't make sense. He and Aislin were mortal enemies.

"Take me to where you last saw her," Alaric demanded, his gaze intent on Kira.

Mikael was suddenly at his side. He glanced at Faas and Aila. "Have Sophie track us once she returns with the others," he ordered.

Kira rose to her feet, recovered from her long run. "Are you ready?" she asked in her small voice.

Both men nodded. Kira took off in the direction she had come with Alaric and Mikael right behind her. Distantly, Alaric could hear Aila shouting orders at Faas, but the words flowed past his ears like an insubstantial breeze. He was faster than any Vaettir he'd encountered over the course of his five hundred years. If those who'd taken Madeline wanted to race, they'd chosen the wrong opponent.

I'D LOST consciousness at some point, and when I awoke, I felt cut off from everything. I couldn't feel the emotions around me, I couldn't sense the banshees, and I couldn't even *see*. Everything was pitch black.

I heard footsteps. I struggled to move, but it felt like I was tied to a wooden chair, each wrist bound to an arm, and each ankle bound to a leg. I could feel the pinch of another rope at my waist.

There was the familiar sound of a matchstick striking its box, then candlelight illuminated the room. Marcos' face became harshly shadowed as he lit several more candles spaced around the area. As the room filled with pockets of light, Estus and Aislin approached from the darkness to stand in front of me.

Estus' dark, loose clothing seemed centuries away from Aislin's prim ballgown, though the pair appeared similar in age and stature. Aislin's expression was blank, while Estus' lined face held a small smile. Marcos moved to stand behind them, his face a pale oval in the deeper shadows of the room.

"Why can't I sense anything?" I rasped, unable to match their silence.

"It's Marcos' gift," Aislin explained, "though he is only able to contend with the charm because you allowed yourself to become so horribly weakened. Even gods need rest."

"I'm not a god," I grumbled, straining against my bonds to no avail.

Estus smirked. "Close enough. The energy of the charm makes you near immortal. It protects you from any that would cause you physical harm."

Remembering his earlier words, I asked, "If that's the case, then how do you intend to cleave it from my soul?"

Estus leaned forward to put his face near mine,

gazing directly into my eyes. "First we will steal the charm from you, *then* we will do the cleaving."

I struggled again, making my hair fall into my face. Frustrated, I tried to blow it away with my mouth, then jerked back as Marcos stepped around Estus to move it for me. Marcos' hand dropped back to his side as he continued to eye me wordlessly, expression unchanged.

I turned my attention back to Estus and Aislin. "Why do you want it so badly?" I asked, trying to stall for time. "If you're working together, then it's obviously not to be the sole leader of the Vaettir."

Estus chuckled. "Since you are about to die, I will explain. No one should go to their grave confused. As you may have noticed, Aislin and I have become rather advanced in age. We are *dying*."

"Everyone dies," I snapped, unable to keep my rage and frustration to myself.

Unfazed, Estus countered, "Not *gods*. With the power of the charm within us, we will be as close to gods as possible. The charm needs its host to live on, and so it will provide us with the power needed to do so."

"Unless someone comes along and takes it away," I argued, "just like you're planning to do with me."

Estus tilted his head and gave me a look of pity. Like he was speaking with a rather dense child, he explained, "The charm will be divided between us. If someone wants it for themselves, they will have to catch us both."

Throbbing pain was building behind my skull. I

needed to keep stalling. For what, I didn't know, but I couldn't just let them kill me.

"Divided?" I questioned. "I don't think that's going to work."

Estus grinned, scaring me. "It will work because our DNA is very similar. Our connection will allow the key to spread its energy between us seamlessly."

My brain came to a skidding halt. "W-wait," I stammered, "your DNA?"

"We're twins," Aislin explained, sounding bored, then added, "Triplets actually, but our sister seems to have met her untimely end."

If my brain had skidded before, now it crashed and exploded in a fiery wave of chaos. I already knew who Aislin's sister was, but had been unaware of her relation to Estus.

"Diana?" I questioned.

Aislin nodded.

I knew I should have had a million questions, but the only one I could think to ask was, "Does James know?"

Aislin eyed me cooly. "He only knows that he was grandson to Diana, who was big my sister, born just a few minutes before me. He does not know of my relation to Estus."

I shook my head over and over. "But if you were just working with your brother from the start, why were you at war? Your people attacked us when I was still at Estus' Salr. The people we questioned, that James *tortured,* were working for *you.*"

Estus chuckled. "What better way to inspire ones troops than to threaten war? What better excuse to question our people for information on the charm, than to claim that they were traitors? The executioner before you had figured it out too. He had conversed with the dead, only to realize *why* I sought the charm. Knowing what fate awaited him, he told others the information he had found. They had to be questioned."

I shook my head and turned my attention to Aislin. "But you wanted me killed. You told your people to kill me as soon as they got the chance."

Aislin smirked. "I did not truly believe the charm was within you, so yes, I wanted you dead, though I did not intend for my people to actually succeed. Their true purpose was simply to locate you. If they died in the process, it would have saved me the trouble of killing them myself."

I squeezed my eyes shut at my own stupidity. "They let you know where we were," I replied. "Even though they expected you to kill them, they still let you know."

Aislin laughed, chilling me to the bone. "They did not betray you. They swore oaths to me. I can sense all of my people at all times. It is my gift."

I turned to Estus. "But you believed the charm was within me? I was told only one of you wanted me dead."

"We want the charm," Estus explained. "We couldn't care less what happens to you afterward. All that matters is that we will be immortal. Still, if you can prove yourself useful after the charm is ours, I would be more than happy to let you live, though I doubt my sister would agree with me."

I shook my head at the senselessness of it all. "So this, *all* of this, was because you were afraid to die?"

"It's more than that," Aislin snapped, her thin lips forming an ugly snarl. "It's what the humans did to us, burning us alive, forcing us into hiding. The Vaettir *need* us to lead them back into the world. To right the wrongs inflicted upon us, so many centuries ago."

I shook my head. "But *you* were the ones keeping the Vaettir underground," I accused.

Estus frowned. "They would have been taken down by the humans eventually. We could not have our people running amuck and getting into trouble before we were prepared. The Vaettir need strong leaders, *invincible* leaders, to reclaim the world for them."

As I reeled over that new thought, I realized Marcos had disappeared. Suddenly I had the idea that perhaps *I* was the one being distracted, and not the other way around. They were giving me the information I wanted to stall me from trying to act.

I focused what little energy I had left inward, searching for the key or for Mara. I felt a distant spark, but it was like I was being blocked from them. It had to be Marcos' doing.

"You're monsters," I grunted, finding no real sense of *anything*. I knew my banshees still had to be out there, likely looking for me, but if Marcos was able to cut me off from the energies *inside* me, it was probably no extra trouble to cut me off from outside ones.

Estus smirked. "Perhaps, but soon we'll be gods."

I shook my head. I knew they were distracting me, but from what? There was nothing I could do.

"So what about me?" I spat. "How did I become a part of this? What about my parents? Did you question and kill them too?"

"Your parents are inconsequential," Estus answered simply. "As you know, our people kept an eye on you while you lived amongst the humans. Over time, some began to expect you were not only an executioner, but an empath. I suspected you were imbued with the Morrigan's energy, but told no one of my suspicions. The Morrigan's energy is special, because she is not truly a god. You are not created in her image, you are *her*. Your lineage doesn't matter. You are likely descended from some common death deity, but your energy is *more*. We had already been searching for the charm for centuries, and I knew if it was going to come forth to anyone, it would be someone with her magic. The key chose you, just as it chose her."

I shook my head, even more confused as Marcos reentered the room, carrying a tray of ritual paraphernalia. I hadn't needed to keep the Morrigan's presence to myself after all. Estus had known all along that I'd been descended from her, and I'd probably only confirmed it for him by revealing I was an empath.

"What do you mean, chose her?" I asked while giving everything I had to fight against Marcos' blockade.

Estus grinned. "The moon has risen overhead, and so the ritual may now begin."

My mouth went dry. The moon? Had I been unconscious an entire day?

Estus smiled knowingly. "Let me tell you one last story before you die, just so you truly understand. When Yggdrasil was destroyed, it formed three things: the Norns, who were the embodiment of fate; the charm, the embodiment of chaotic energy and wild magics; and the Morrigan, who had formed the roots of the tree. She was the earth, and the balance between all things.

"When the parts of the tree were torn apart, they naturally wanted to go back together. The charm found the Morrigan, imbuing her with great powers. Many thought she was a god, though she wasn't. She came into existence long after the old gods had left the world of man. Still, together the charm and the Morrigan were unstoppable. She would have ruled over this earth even today, if she had not been overcome by human emotions.

"For within the Morrigan was the balance of life and death, dark and light, and all the emotions that drive the never ending cycles. She fell in love, and was betrayed. She turned to darkness, throwing off the balance that was part of her very being. It destroyed her, casting her energy out into the universe."

"No," I whispered. It was all too much. Why hadn't Mara told me?

"Yes," Estus replied. "When I realized just what you were, I knew the time had come. You were born to return balance, but you are too weak, too *human* for the job. My sister and I will have to take it from here."

"Enough talk," Aislin snapped. "We must complete the ritual while the moon is still fresh in the sky."

My heart raced. That was it. They'd been stalling until nightfall. I tried with all of my might to summon enough energy just to get them away from me, but it was no use. Marcos approached with the tray. On it sat an ornate dagger, what looked like a chalice of blood or some other dark liquid, and two lit candles, one white and one black.

He kneeled before me and set the tray on the ground as Estus and Aislin both took a step back.

Marcos lifted the dagger from the tray, and before I could even react, he sliced open my forearm, still tied to the arm of the chair. A moment later, the wound began to sting as blood poured forth. He lifted the chalice to my dripping blood, letting it mingle with the dark liquid already residing within.

"With the blood of the fates, I call you forth, *lykill*," Marcos chanted, using the old Norsk term for the key.

I panted in fear as his words flowed over me. *The blood of the fates.* If the Norns were the fates, did that mean . . . it all suddenly made sense. He hadn't killed the Norns who'd sent us back in time just to rob them of their energy. He'd needed their blood to call to the key. They were the other severed part of

Yggdrasil. The key would naturally want to join with them.

He handed the chalice, now containing an ample amount of my blood to mix with the Norns', back to Aislin, who took a hearty swallow.

I gagged at the sight. Not only was she drinking *blood*, but half of it had been lying around for several weeks.

Next, she handed the chalice to Estus, who downed the rest of the liquid, leaving a red stain on his lips as he lowered the vessel. Estus crouched to return the chalice to the tray, then took up the candles, handing the black one to Aislin, while keeping the white for himself.

Marcos glanced back at them, then to me. "With the balance of light and dark, I call you."

He placed his hands on either side of my ribcage, and I began to feel a pulling sensation, much like how it felt when Faas drained my energy. The first sign I had that the key was even still inside of me at all, was its sudden reaction to the ritual. It was being called forth.

I gasped as the enormous energy of the key suddenly gushed outward through my skin. There was nothing to see with our eyes, but it felt like molten metal was flooding out of my pores. Marcos pulled his hands away, and they glowed with energy.

"I cannot remove every trace from her," he said through gritted teeth, "but it should be enough."

Still kneeling, he turned his upper body toward Estus and Aislin. They each took one of his hands, with the candles held in their free palms.

I could sense the energy as it transferred to them, and suddenly I could sense everything else too. Aislin and Estus threw their heads back in identical expressions of rapture while Marcos bowed before them. The transfer of energies seemed to be taking all of Marcos' attention, because his mental hold on me had loosened. Before I could act, Mara's energy rushed forth, jumping into the nearest target, Marcos.

In the blink of an eye, Marcos stood, grabbing the dagger from the tray on his way up. While Aislin and Estus were still overcome by the euphoria of their newly acquired power, Marcos shoved the dagger into the bodice of Aislin's dress, searching upward for her heart.

She screamed as her body collapsed, and blood blossomed on the white fabric of her dress like a red rose in winter. The candle flames flickered from the abrupt movements as Marcos withdrew the blade, leaving Aislin sputtering on the ground. He turned to where Estus had been, but he was already backing away, looking down at his sister's corpse.

Estus smiled coldly, then met my eyes, not seeming to view Marcos as a threat. "I never liked sharing power anyhow," he muttered, then turned and ran, far too nimble for a man of his apparent age.

I expected Marcos, possessed by Mara, to follow him, but his body began to quiver as he dropped back to his knees before me. The dagger clattered to the floor beside him as his hands gripped my thighs almost painfully. His head bowed near my lap.

"I don't have much longer," he said, turning his gaze upward to meet my eyes. "This body still has a soul, and I am too weak to maintain my hold. My time here is through."

Though I was looking down at a man, Mara's fierce energy shone through his gray eyes. I wanted to reach out to cradle his face, but my hands were still bound.

Suddenly Alaric and Mikael came crashing into the room, followed by Faas.

"What the—" Faas began, just as Alaric leapt toward Marcos.

"No!" I shouted, stopping him mid-motion.

I looked back down to Marcos as he lifted a hand to cradle my face instead. "You are so much stronger than I ever was," he whispered. "I know you will complete the cycle. You will restore balance, where I failed."

Marcos slumped onto my lap as Mara's energy left him. I couldn't tell if he was unconscious or dead, and I didn't really care. Mara was gone. I was now alone in my body for the first time in what seemed like years. I should have been ecstatic, but all I could feel was loss.

Alaric took a step forward while Mikael and Faas stood back. Not asking questions, he gently pushed Marcos aside, allowing him to slump down to the floor before he began untying my bonds. He tensed as he noticed my bloody arm, but continued his work.

When I was free, he helped me stand, and I *needed* the help. Despite all that had happened, I'd still been drained of energy, and I'd still gone two nights without sleep. Faas wasn't the only one who'd weakened me to the point of vulnerability. I'd done just as much damage myself.

As I leaned against Alaric, we both looked down at Aislin. She was still alive, though blood splattered out of her mouth as she tried to breath, lying immobile on her back.

"Do we let her die?" Mikael questioned. There was a wicked smile on his face, as if he was very pleased with the notion.

I looked down at Aislin, for the first time feeling absolutely no sympathy for someone's death. I could distantly feel her pain, but it was nothing compared to the enormous loss I felt within me. Emotional pain trumps physical pain without fail.

"Everything dies," I answered coldly as I stared at Aislin's bloody chest.

Her eyes darted around the room frantically until they met mine. I instructed Alaric to help me kneel beside her and added, "Even gods," just as I placed my hand on her cheek and stole her life away.

17

Stealing Aislin's energy gave me a measure of strength, but I was still painfully weary. Alaric helped me back to my feet to face Mikael and Fass.

"Estus was here," I explained.

"I thought I smelled him," Alaric growled, maintaining a tight grip around my waist.

"He took the key," I added, not sure how I felt about that fact.

Marcos had claimed that some of the key's energy still remained inside me, though I couldn't sense it, nor could I sense any lingering energy from Mara.

Faas gasped, then looked me up and down. "I sense traces of its energy, but it's more like part of you, not a foreign entity. How is that possible?"

I shrugged. I had an idea, but nothing was concrete. "One of the Norns once told me she could transfer the key from me to my child. Marcos used the blood of the

Norn's he helped kill for the ritual. They are the fates, part of Yggdrasil, so their blood calls to the key."

"Marcos?" Alaric questioned softly.

I turned partially to look down at the executioner. I could see the rise and fall of his chest. Just unconscious then, not dead. *Pity.*

"So you're free," Alaric muttered in awe as we all stared down at Marcos.

"But Estus has the key," I added.

Alaric turned to me, grabbing both my arms in his so I would meet his eyes directly. "This doesn't have to be your fight anymore."

What I was about to say made me want to cry, but I had to say it. "I made a promise. This is my fight until the bitter end."

Mikael stepped into view. "Do not do this just for Erykah. I will find Estus and avenge her myself."

I could sense the truth in his words. He would go after Estus and the key, even if it meant his death.

I shook my head. "Erykah wasn't the only one I made a promise to. I have to set things right." I turned back to Alaric. "I will *not* bring my child into a world where Estus is the omnipotent leader. He wants to enact vengeance against all of mankind. The death of one tyrant has not ended this war."

Alaric pulled me close, wrapping his arms tightly around me. I almost thought he was crying, but when he pulled away, his eyes were dry.

Still, his tortured expression made my heart hurt. "It will be okay," I soothed.

He nodded. "I know."

A tear did slip down his face then.

I lifted a finger and wiped it away. "Then why are you sad?"

He smiled despite his tears and pulled me into another crushing hug. His body moved with laughter as he held me close. "The moment that you said you still had to fight, not out of vengeance, but because it's the right thing to do. In that moment, I knew you were fully yourself again. Part of me thought I had lost you."

I wrapped my arms around him and squeezed just as tightly as I let out a few tears of my own. "Did you really think that small things like the root of chaos and an ancient deity could keep me away from you?" I joked.

He stroked my hair, still holding me tight. "Not for a moment, but it's a relief either way."

"Oh enough cuddling," someone said from behind us.

I pulled away from Alaric enough to see Sophie clattering down a set of stairs leading into the room, which led me to actually look around the rest of the room. It wasn't a Salr, that much was clear. The room just looked like a plain old cellar, except for the corpse and the blood everywhere.

Sophie was followed by Aila, and both of Aislin's people, whose names I was yet to catch.

I lost my breath as I suddenly recalled just how I'd fallen into Estus' and Aislin's hands.

"Where is James?" I asked weakly.

I was met with silence.

I looked to Sophie, knowing she of all people would be brutally honest with me.

"He finally got what he deserved," she said coldly.

One of Aislin's people, the man with coppery skin and long dark hair, stepped around us to look at his former Doyen. He nudged the arm of her corpse with the toe of his boot, making it flop lifelessly.

"She's much less scary this way," he commented. His eyes met mine. "I owe you for my newfound freedom, and will help you if I can, but I do not desire a new leader."

"Nor do I," the female chimed in, keeping her distance, "though I'm also grateful."

I looked to Mikael, Faas, and Aila, who now stood side by side.

"Well you know *I'm* not going anywhere," Mikael teased.

Aila sighed, but nodded her assent, while Faas smiled softly.

"To the bitter end?" I questioned.

Mikael reached out his hand with a wry grin. Smiling, I put my hand on top of his. Alaric followed suit, then came Aila and Faas. With a sigh loud enough to make sure everyone knew how annoyed she was, Sophie marched across the room and slapped her hand down on top of Faas'.

"To the *bitter* end," she sighed.

We all echoed her, pushing our palms down before lifting them all up in unison.

"The fellowship lives!" Mikael exclaimed.

I laughed at the *Lord of the Rings* reference as one of Aislin's people muttered to the other, "What have we gotten ourselves into?"

Alaric suddenly pulled me aside. Staying within his grasp, I turned to see Marcos climbing to his feet, using the chair I'd been tied to for balance.

Mikael came to stand on my other side, observing the executioner. "Do we kill him?"

I gritted my teeth as I glared at Marcos, who now stood silently, bravely awaiting his fate. "We might need him to tear the key out of Estus."

"But will he cooperate?" Mikael asked quizzically, continuing to speak about Marcos like he wasn't even there.

The necromancer's face remained stony. I couldn't sense a single drop of emotion from him. He was either capable of completely shutting me out, or he just didn't feel anything.

I sighed, feeling guilty because I kind of wished Marcos had just died in all of the commotion, making the tough decision for us. The memory of the Morrigan looking out at me from his eyes was still fresh on my mind, making me feel a measure of compassion toward him that I shouldn't have.

Plus, he'd been able to block me from my banshees, so he was dangerous . . . but perhaps it had only been since I was so weakened. Would he be able to do it now that I'd regained my strength from Aislin's energy.

I startled. Mara was gone. Did I even still have banshees? They were supposed to be under *my* command, so I should. The thought of them frightened me now that I was more myself, but we still needed an upper hand against Estus. Using the Norn's blood, he'd lured the key into himself. I wasn't sure if the key would work for him now, but it would still want to survive. Now that it was in Estus' body, it would *need* him to survive as well.

First thing was first though, I needed to see if the phantoms would still answer my call.

I pulled away from Alaric and headed for the stairs. As I approached, a gust of fresh air hit me, drawing my gaze to the stars above.

Alaric appeared behind me a moment later as I climbed the stairs out into the moonlight.

I took in our surroundings, since I'd been unconscious when I'd first entered the cellar. Sparse trees surrounded us, and to my left was an old homestead, long since fallen into disrepair.

Alaric and I stepped forward as the rest of our party joined us. Mikael and Aila came to stand beside me, each holding on to one of Marcos' arms. Suddenly I felt like maybe we *should* kill him. If I was still able to call to the banshees, he might try to take control of them. I had no idea what necromancers were capable of.

Alaric wrapped his arm around my shoulders as he said, "You should probably wait on certain *things* until we have this one locked away." He nodded toward Marcos.

I nodded in agreement, though it would be hard to wait. I really wanted to know how much Mara's departure had affected our plans.

Suddenly a shiver of what felt like electricity zinged down my spine. Alaric pulled his arm away as if he'd felt it too.

"What was that?" he asked warily.

I gasped as I realized what I was sensing. "Get Marcos away from here," I ordered breathlessly.

Mikael and Aila began to tug him away, but it was too late. The air grew even colder as dark shapes darted between us and the moon. The banshees were still around, and they'd found me.

They descended as we all stood in awe. I wasn't sure if they would listen to me now that Mara was gone, but it was our only hope.

The banshees reached the ground and surrounded us, accompanied by other phantoms, their nightmare shapes only perceivable in my peripheral vision.

We are sorry, my queen, a voice echoed through my head. *We could not find you.*

I heaved a sigh of relief, and could sense Alaric relaxing beside me, though he hadn't heard the voice.

You are different, my queen, another banshee with a deeper voice observed.

I cringed, and just as my mind flitted across the fact that Mara and the key had left me, the banshees suddenly knew, just as they knew my fears that they would no longer follow me.

You are who we followed, the first one who'd spoken explained. *You called us from the earth, and only you can return us.*

I sighed again. We had a chance. We could do this. The key might have been all powerful, but an army of phantoms was nothing to laugh at either. We would hunt Estus down and restore balance, no matter the cost. It was the least I could do, now that Mara was gone.

Before I could explain to my living companions that we were in the clear, I felt something tugging at my consciousness. No, it was tugging at the phantoms.

I felt sick as I remembered Marcos. I'd been so consumed with my inner dialogue I'd almost forgotten my initial fears. They were coming to life now as he tried to steal my phantoms.

My eyes met his. Aila and Mikael had stopped their movements when the banshees appeared, and didn't seem able to sense what Marcos was doing. It made sense. They had no affiliation with the dead. This struggle was between Marcos and I alone.

A small, knowing smile curved the necromancer's lips.

Ever perceptive, even if he couldn't feel the dead, Mikael asked, "Is he doing something that he shouldn't be doing? I'll gladly kill him."

"No," I answered. "I mean yes, but don't kill him."

I was no longer a scared little mouse, and this man was not stronger than me. I repeated the words like a mantra in my head, willing them to be true as I marched up to where Marcos stood, sandwiched between Mikael and Aila.

His smile faltered, only to be replaced by his normal, stony expression. He gasped as I shut my shields into place, cutting him off from *my* phantoms.

I came to stand before him, feeling smug. "I was weakened when you found me," I explained, looking up since he was several inches taller than me.

I was close enough to invade his personal bubble, but he couldn't back away from Mikael and Aila's iron grips.

"And you may have taken the key from me," I continued.

A small measure of his sudden fear leaked through, then was shut away as he realized it.

"But *I*," I went on, "am not weak. I am the Morrigan incarnate, and lowly necromancers like you should be bowing at my feet."

He audibly gulped, surprising me almost as much as I'd just surprised myself.

Mikael raised an eyebrow at me. "Are you *sure* the Morrigan left you?"

I smiled as I turned to walk back to my waiting banshees, then thought better of it. My smile still in place, I spun back around and punched Marcos in the face.

The impact reeled him backward, and the only thing that kept him from falling was Mikael's grip as Aila stepped back.

"*That's* for kidnapping me and cutting my arm open," I said evenly.

Righting himself, Marcos nodded. "Yes, my queen," he said evenly.

Oh good grief, I thought, turning away as I tried to slow my speeding heart. Sophie had joined Alaric, and they were both grinning at me. Aislin's minions, whose names I would have to learn at some point, just looked scared.

Ignoring them, I approached Alaric.

"Permission to kiss you, *my queen*?" he asked jokingly.

"Permission granted," I replied.

As Alaric leaned in for a kiss, I heard one of Aislin's people whisper, "I think they're *crazy*."

I laughed, then Alaric smothered my lips with his. I wrapped my arms around his neck, not caring that we had strangers and a gaggle of banshees watching us, and kissed him for all I was worth.

See? I told you I'm no creampuff.

18

We retreated back to the Salr. I hoped Kira wouldn't mind the extra company. Something told me she'd be okay with it.

We took Marcos with us. It was a dangerous move to leave him alive, but I didn't want to risk losing a possibly useful resource. We needed all the resources we could get.

He hadn't spoken a word since the scene outside the cellar, but had come with us willingly. Something told me he had an entire internal plot of his own, but there was nothing I could do about it short of killing him, so we would just have to wait and see.

The main reason I wanted Marcos around was simple. If we could capture Estus, then maybe Marcos would be able to transfer the key back to me. I hadn't voiced to anyone yet that this was my hope, since they would all call me crazy. Maybe I was. All I knew was that

I would need the key to restore balance. I would also need the Morrigan's energy, the energy of the earth, which hopefully I possessed on my own. The final piece was fate. All of Mikael's Norns had been killed, but there had to still be some out there, and we would need to find them.

Once I had gathered all of those pieces, I would hopefully know what to do. Mara had claimed I would know. I wasn't sure if I would regrow Yggdrasil, or if putting all of those energies together would be enough to achieve anything of worth. Really, I didn't know much at all. At the moment I was just grateful to be back with my friends, in a relatively safe, warm environment, my belly filled with food, and my skin draped in silky blue pajamas.

I rolled over in bed to see Alaric, who had apparently been watching me as I mulled over my thoughts.

He reached out a hand and stroked my hair. "You know Estus might come back here for you."

I smiled. "Let him. It would save us the trouble of finding him."

"You truly think you can subdue him, even though he now has the key?" he pressed.

I placed my hand over his and brought it to rest against my cheek. "Your worry is making me anxious," I teased.

He smiled. "You know, teasing in dire situations is supposed to be *my* thing."

I snuggled a little closer. "The banshees will come to

my call the moment I step foot outside. Mara, the Morrigan," I corrected, realizing Alaric didn't know her true name, "was a force equal to the key. The key was chaos, and she was the earth, and the balance between all things."

"But you're not *her*," he countered.

I frowned. "No, but I'm all we've got. Plus Marcos and the banshees."

"That's the other thing," he sighed. "I think we should have killed Marcos. He was able to block you from calling the phantoms, and he tried to call them from you, even after he'd been captured."

"And he failed," I added.

"This time," he argued.

I rolled onto my back, pulling away from him. "You really have no faith in me, do you?"

He turned and wrapped his arms around my ribcage, pulling me back toward him, then propped himself up so he could look at me. "Madeline, you are the *only* thing I have faith in."

I smiled. "Then trust me on this."

He leaned forward and laid a gentle kiss on my lips, but seemed perplexed as he pulled away.

Suddenly worried, I asked, "What is it?"

He frowned. "I just realized you never told me what it was you were trying to hide from the key. Why you couldn't say all that you needed to while it was still inside you."

My heart warmed. "So you understood? I was hoping

you would. It was so hard trying to leave without being able to explain."

He gave me a tight squeeze. "I understood you couldn't say certain things in front of the key, not what they were."

I smiled, content in the fact that Alaric had known me well enough to understand what I'd been trying to convey. "The Morrigan and I were working with the key, with the intent of regrowing Yggdrasil."

Alaric tensed, but didn't speak.

"What the key didn't understand, was that it would have to become a part of the tree again, and hence, a part of the earth. It would no longer be a sentient being."

Alaric nodded in understanding. "So you wanted to keep the key in favor of your plan. If you'd told me you were going to regrow Yggdrasil, I would have questioned you, and you might have said the wrong thing."

"Exactly," I replied.

"But that doesn't explain why you wouldn't let me help you," he countered. "I would have gone along, even without an explanation."

I sighed. "That was the Morrigan's side of the deal, that I needed to do things on my own. I couldn't be distracted by wanting to keep you safe."

"So you were shielding certain things from the Morrigan too," he said.

I cringed.

He raised a dark eyebrow at me. "Or maybe you weren't?"

I let out a long breath, preparing myself to be honest. "I agreed with her. I would have never been able to go around raising spirits from their graves if I was worried about you coming to harm."

"And?" he pressed, knowing me too well to let the explanation drop at that.

"And," I continued, "I needed to prove to myself that I could do it on my own. My entire life I've run from things. I've run from my past, from love, and even from *you*. I don't want our daughter to ever feel like she can't handle things on her own. I need to be a living example of that."

Alaric laid a gentle kiss on my temple, then held me close. "Our *daughter*," he mused. "I still can't get used to it."

I smiled. "So you forgive me for leaving you out of things?"

He chuckled. "There is nothing to forgive. It was always your choice to make, as much as I would have liked to fight against it."

I smiled and relaxed into his embrace as I rubbed a hand across my belly. "I'm glad my daughter will have a father that won't tell her she can't do things on her own."

His hand covered mine to feel the small bump underneath the fabric of my pajamas. "Oh I'll try," he joked, "but with the perfect role model of her mother around, I doubt I'll have much luck."

"So you're fine with her being just like me?" I asked slyly.

He laughed. "I'm fine with her being whatever she wants, as long as she's not too much like my sister."

I jumped as the door to our room suddenly flew open to reveal Sophie, standing in the doorway with her hip cocked, and a bottle of champagne in her hand.

"That's not very nice, *brother*," she chided.

Mikael appeared in the doorway behind her with a paper shopping bag in each hand.

Sophie entered the room uninvited, then came to sit on the foot of our bed while Alaric and I moved to seated positions. Alaric let out a long sigh.

I combed my fingers through my hair to make sure I didn't look like too much of a mess, but gave up. When people like Sophie and Mikael barged into your room, you had little choice but to go along with it. I raised an eyebrow at the bags in Mikael's hands as he approached us.

"We're never letting the Viking do the supply shopping again," Sophie commented as Mikael set the bags on the bedside table. "It's almost all booze," she added, lifting the champagne bottle in her hand for emphasis.

"Well I for one think we deserve to celebrate," Mikael teased, removing a bottle of whiskey from the bag, followed by a package of plastic cups.

He handed me the cups while Alaric glared at him, then produced another champagne bottle from the bag, handing it to me.

"Sparkling cider," he explained, "for little Mikaela junior," he added, gesturing to my belly.

"Hah *hah*," I replied sarcastically, tearing open the plastic encasing the cups. "Where are Aila and the others?"

"Watching our new friend Marcos to make sure he doesn't get any funny ideas," Mikael explained as he pulled the corked top out of the whiskey.

I smirked. "Maybe we should invite him too. He might be nicer when he's drunk."

Alaric looked at me seriously, for once the only one in the conversation *not* joking.

I offered him a smile as I handed him the sparkling cider to uncork.

He rolled his eyes then smiled, giving in to the situation. He popped the cork into his hand, then took the cup I handed him to pour me a glass. After handing the filled cup and bottle back to me, he accepted a cup of champagne from Sophie. I scooted closer to Alaric and leaned against the headboard beside him. He put his arm around me obligingly, and I felt it as the tension drained from him.

Whiskey in hand, Mikael stood before us and raised his glass. "To traveling through time, cavorting with deities, getting possessed and unpossessed, and still coming out alive."

I lifted my glass. "To the living, to the dead, and to fate herself."

Alaric lifted his glass toward the center of the group, but his eyes were all for me as he said, "To Madeline, for being both strong and kind, light and dark, and everything in between, *and* to our daughter, who will not be named Mikaela."

Sophie snorted at Alaric's toast, then lifted her glass. "To family," she said, encompassing both Alaric and I in her gaze, "and to friends, sort of," she added, looking to Mikael, who accepted the inclusion with a slight bow, "and to James," she sighed, "may he find peace in death, even if he doesn't deserve it."

We all touched the rims of our glasses, then took a sip. Well, Mikael took more than a sip, then poured himself another glass.

I snuggled closer to Alaric and placed a hand on my belly, enjoying the simple moment. I felt like I'd quite literally been through hell and back, and maybe, just maybe, I was better for the experience.

It was odd to think about how my life had been before, living alone in my little house, avoiding close relationships. Avoiding *life*. Now I not only had friends, but I had a true partner in Alaric, and eventually we would have a daughter.

What were a few unparalleled forces of nature to contend with, when you had rewards like those?

NOTE FROM THE AUTHOR

I hope you've enjoyed reading the third installment in the Bitter Ashes Series!

For news and updates, please sign up for my mailing list by visiting:

www.saracroethle.com

SNEAK PEEK AT BOOK FOUR

DUCK, DUCK, NOOSE

I frowned across the table at Marcos, the executioner of my now dead enemy, Aislin. His long, pure white hair hung forward as he looked down at the coffee cup I had placed in front of him. I'd figured a little civility could go a long way, but apparently I'd figured wrong.

He hadn't touched the hot beverage, something that pissed me off more than it should, based solely on the fact that I couldn't have any. Alaric had assured me that because I'm Vaettir, caffeine, rough-housing, or even radiation wouldn't be able to hurt my baby, but I couldn't bring myself to drink it. I'd been raised amongst humans, and some practices would stay with me forever.

"Where did you learn to transfer energies?" I demanded for the hundredth time as I shifted in my seat and tugged my soft, gray sweater down over the small bump of my belly.

Marcos simply stared at me.

Alejandro snorted. I turned back to see him leaning against the stone wall behind me, looking admittedly scrumptious with his long, black hair draped around his strong Native American features. He'd also been one of Aislin's people, but I liked him better. He'd been more than happy to come to my side. Of course, that probably had more to do with the fact that she'd intended to kill him than anything else.

Alejandro had been assigned Marcos guard duty since we'd first arrived back at the Salr originally shown to me by the Morrigan. Alejandro's usual partner was Aila, since we didn't necessarily trust him to be alone with Tallie and Marcos, both formerly Aislin's people. Now that Aislin was dead, they didn't have much reason to betray us, but better safe than sorry.

When Alejandro and Aila needed rest, either Mikael and Tallie, or Sophie and Alaric would take over on guard duty. Since apparently being pregnant made me an invalid, I didn't get to guard anyone. Of course, Faas didn't get to stand guard either, mainly because Marcos, as a true necromancer, was more than a match for his powers as an executioner. Fass was capable of draining a person's energy, which was a scary trait to have, but Marcos had proven his skills at energy manipulation were superior.

Alejandro flipped his hair over his shoulder, show-casing his strong cheekbones and dark eyes. His crimson tee shirt made his skin stand out in rich contrast. "He's not going to tell you anything. He's been Aislin's pet for over a century." He sneered at Marcos. "Probably mourning the loss of his little tyrant queen."

"I mourn the loss of no one," Marcos interjected.

Alejandro and I jumped at the sound of his voice. He hadn't spoken since we'd brought him to the Salr, and I had begun to think he never would.

I turned and raised an eyebrow at him. He still had a fading bruise on his cheek from my fist, but the rest of his face was like a pale, smooth stone. His expression gave nothing away.

I sighed at his renewed silence. "And here I thought we were about to become friends."

He tilted his head. "We can become *friends*, Phantom Queen, but I will not confide information in front of the traitor." His eyes flicked to Alejandro.

I narrowed my eyes at him. "Then we'll find a different guard."

Marcos shook his head. "We speak alone, or not at all."

"Why?" I pressed, pushing my wavy hair away from my face, only to have it fall forward again.

He pursed his lips. "There are certain things that only *you* will understand. I would not have your opinion instantly swayed by the words of others, before you've had the time to decide yourself."

Well now I was intrigued. "Fine," I snapped.

"Maddy-" Alejandro began, but I cut him off with a sharp look.

He didn't seem happy about it, but went to the door,

opened it, and exited the small room. Aila peeked her head in from the hallway after Alejandro passed, likely wondering why I hadn't followed him out.

"We need a moment," I told her.

She raised both eyebrows in surprise high enough that I thought they might touch the hairline of her white-blonde ponytail. "Mikael expressly demanded that you not be left alone with him." She nodded in Marcos' direction.

"You'll just be right outside the door," I said sweetly.

Aila frowned. "If you come to harm, I'm blaming Alejandro."

"Hey!" Alejandro called from somewhere behind her, but Aila shut the door before I could hear whatever snide remark he likely had for her.

I turned back to Marcos. "Happy?"

He smiled a wicked smile, making me suddenly regret my decision. "You're very trusting for someone who's been narrowly escaping death for the past month," he observed.

I gave him a patient smile in an attempt to hide my anxiety, then aimed my eyes at the bruise on his face. "I think I've already proven I'm not afraid of you."

He nodded in acceptance. "Touché, nor have you any reason to be. To answer your original question, I'm descended from the goddess Hecate. My ability to shift energy wasn't something I learned. It is a talent I've always possessed."

I'd heard of the goddess Hecate, and knew she was

248

associated with necromancy, so it made sense. One thing didn't though. "And why did we need to be alone for you to tell me that?"

"We didn't, but I wasn't sure if you wanted the others to know just what you're planning."

I inhaled sharply. There was no way for him to know. The exact details of my plan had remained between the Morrigan and myself. I'd filled Alaric in on as much as I could, and he knew the gist of my plan, but I'd sworn that certain things I would keep secret.

"I've been inside your head, Madeline," he taunted. "Don't play dumb."

I exhaled and did my best to relax. He was referring to when he'd taken the key from me. He'd connected with my energy in order to separate it from the key, but if he caught a glimpse of anything else, it was brief. "What exactly is it that you think you know?"

"You're going to regrow Yggdrasil," he stated. "You're going to bridge the gap between the mundane world and the gods. In effect, you'll be releasing magic to affect the lives of mortals."

So maybe he did know my plan. "The only way to defeat the key is to return it to its natural state. It needs to be reunited with the earth, time, and fate. But first, it has to be reunited with *me*."

A knock sounded on the door, then Alejandro poked his head in. "Everything alright?"

"We're fine," I said quickly, praying he hadn't overheard anything. Alaric at least knew that I wanted to regrow Ygdrassil, but he didn't know that I wanted the key back.

Alejandro shut the door, and I turned back to Marcos.

"Why don't you want them to know?" he questioned.

"They don't trust the Morrigan," I explained. "If they knew the exact plan she came up with, they'd simply think it's her way of returning to this world for another reign of terror."

He smirked. "And is it?"

I frowned. "No, it's not."

He laughed, and finally took a sip of his coffee, though it was likely cold by now. "Are you sure?"

"Her energy lived inside me for a time, as you know," I explained. "She had no malicious intent. Now why all of the sudden interest?"

He took another sip of his cooling coffee. "You managed to beat me at my own game. This interest is anything *but* sudden."

I frowned, thinking back to when he'd tried to steal my banshees from me. It hadn't been difficult to break his connection with them, but it scared me none-the-less. Next time I might not be so lucky, and without the key or the Morrigan, the banshees were the only ace in the hole I had left.

I sighed. "Let me rephrase. Why are you suddenly speaking with me so candidly?"

"My goddess has bid me to do so," he replied simply.

I cleared my throat in an attempt to hide my sudden

discomfort. "You're talking to me because Hecate told you to?"

He nodded. "Is that so odd? You had your goddess *inside* of you."

I took a shaky breath, thinking of Mara. She'd technically been *inside* Marcos too, using his body to kill Aislin. "The Morrigan wasn't exactly a goddess," I explained. "She told me the old gods no longer answer the calls of their children."

"You know, many view Hecate and the Morrigan as the same incarnation of the *dark goddess*," he said conversationally.

I frowned. "But they're not. I *met* the Morrigan, and I highly doubt she's whispering in your ear right now."

He chuckled. "You are correct. My point is, Hecate isn't like the old gods either. She is an incarnation of the dark goddess, just as the Morrigan was, just as others were before her. Kali is another good example. They were all individuals, yet they were composed of the same energy, existing at different times."

I eyed Marcos' coffee, seriously wishing I had a cup after that whopper of an info-dump. "Please get to the point," I said tiredly, not wanting to admit that all the things he was talking about were beyond my comprehension.

Marcos rolled his eyes. "Hecate can speak to me because she's like the Morrigan. She is the earth itself, light and dark, life and death. She never *fully* leaves this world, because she's too much a part of it."

I narrowed my eyes at him. "If all of this is true, why are you not an empath, and why am I not a true necromancer?"

Marcos sighed and began tracing the table's wood-grain with his finger absentmindedly. "Kali, Hecate, the Morrigan, and all other embodiments of the dark goddess were still individual women with their own affinities. Hecate was the daughter of Titans, giving her power over the sea, and she was also a true necromancer, traveling freely to the spirit underworld. The Morrigan, I'm told, was created when Yggdrasil was destroyed. The Norns became the keepers of time and fate. The charm, or the key, as you call it, became the wild magic and chaos that pushes everything forward. The Morrigan was left with all the rest, including emotion. Hence, empathy."

My eyes widened, not because he'd told me something new, but because very few knew that story. Had he gleaned it when he'd taken the key from me, or had Hecate really told him? I bit my lip, realizing another option. *Estus.* He'd known that I was connected to the Morrigan, and knew that she had previously possessed the key.

I glanced at the door behind us, knowing we'd likely have another visit from Alejandro soon, or worse, Alaric or Mikael would realize that I was alone in a room with Marcos.

"While this is all highly informative," I began evenly, wishing I could quiz him for information for hours, "I still don't understand your motivation for speaking with me."

He'd been looking down at his hand, still tracing along the wood grain, but now smiled up at me through a curtain of pure white hair. "Hecate believes in your cause, and would like to assist in your purpose."

I shook my head. "And just like that, you'll give up any allegiance you had to Aislin?"

He smirked. "I've no allegiance to anyone, nor does Hecate. Aislin sought the charm, and so I followed out of convenience."

"Then why aren't you trying to run to Estus' waiting arms right now?" I countered.

Marcos frowned. "I want the charm, not a ruler, and Estus will not be so easily overcome. His power lies in diplomacy, and in making his people adore him. Now that he has what he wants, he will be fortifying his empire. We need to plan carefully."

"We?" I asked.

"You and I," he clarified. "We have the same goals. It's only natural we should work together."

I narrowed my eyes at him. "No offense, but less than a week ago you helped kidnap me. You tied me to a chair, cut open my arm, and stole the key from me. I'm not feeling terribly trusting right now."

He chuckled. "And you would not have done the same to me, had the positions been reversed?"

I smirked. "I don't know, but here you are sitting in a

chair without ropes, sipping coffee. I don't remember being offered any coffee when I was at *your* mercy."

He offered a smug smile. "Yes, I suppose you could have attempted to torture this information out of me. Or you could have starved me until I was too weak to deny your bidding."

I smiled sweetly. "Exactly, so please don't compare me to yourself."

He nodded. "Point taken, but the fact still stands, you *need* me to transfer the charm's energy, and you also need a plan to bring us to that point. As you witnessed, the transfer takes time and ritual. We'll need to create a situation where we can separate Estus from his people, in order to subdue him long enough to regain the charm."

I sighed. "And how do you propose we do all of this?"

Marcos' eyes met mine. "We must make you Doyen of the remaining Vaettir not yet under Estus' rule. The best way to conquer an empire, is to build a stronger one."

My jaw fell. There was a knock at the door, then Alaric's head poked in. "What the hell is going on here?" he asked, his attention one hundred percent on me.

I glanced at Marcos, then back to Alaric. "Making new friends?" I said hopefully.

Alaric frowned, then let out an exaggerated sigh. "Of *course* you are, because a pain in the ass Viking and the little nymph Kira that hides in rooms and eavesdrops on conversations aren't enough, let's add our enemy's pet necromancer to the gang."

I remained in my seat and smiled nervously up at him as he came the rest of the way into the room. "Just one big, happy family?" I asked, half-joking.

His expression softened as he looked down at me with a loving smile, though his eyes still held worry. "Madeline, you've somehow acquired an exceedingly dark sense of humor."

I smiled. "I learned from the best."

Marcos watched our interaction curiously.

As if just remembering that we had company, Alaric offered me a hand up out of my seat.

I turned to Marcos, unsure of what else to say. "I'll get back to you," I said finally, leaving it at that.

"One last thing," he said, just as I was turning to leave.

Alaric and I turned back to him.

"You've weakened your banshees to a dangerous point," he stated bluntly. "They need a constant source of energy to survive. They need to feed off the dead, and you've denied them all sustenance. Do not let your best form of defense whither into nothing."

I frowned. He was right. I'd spent as little time around the banshees as possible, and I hadn't visited any more graveyards. It wasn't that I was ungrateful for the help they offered, but they scared me. When I was with them at full power, it was almost overwhelming, and I became something I wasn't. I was afraid to feel that again, and even more afraid that next time, maybe I wouldn't come back from it.

I nodded. "I'll keep that in mind, and I will let you know what we decide regarding your proposal."

He smiled, and it for some reason made me nervous. He'd known a whole hell of a lot about my plans, and now I was considering letting him in on even more. I didn't have much of a choice, really. Marcos was an integral part of the process.

So why did I feel like I was stepping off a ledge?

Marcos held his arms wide to encompass the small room. "I'll be waiting, obviously."

He'd be waiting all right, with his dark goddess whispering in his ear all the while.

Made in the USA
Coppell, TX
25 October 2019

10417684R10142